One story's ending is just another's beginning.

Cari Lyn Jones

The Broken Court

Lapis Moon Publishing

The Broken Court

The sequel novella to
Lumina and The Goblin King

written by Cari Lyn Jones

Table of Contents

Henwife, spaewife, wise woman, witch…

You see her in many fairy tales –

She is the herb woman who gives the heroine just what is needed to escape her dire fate.

The old woman in the cottage at the edge of a dark wood who advises the hero on which path to take.

She is the giver of good advice and the keeper of secret knowledge. The wise crone who guides the maiden, helping her to win love and happiness.

She is *not* the one who finds love and happiness herself… but why shouldn't she be?

On a side note, although *The Broken Court* can stand on its own, it will be much more enjoyable (and make a great deal more sense) if you have read the first book in the series, *Lumina and the Goblin King*.

After All is Said and Done

The wedding was done and the night now lay in soft folds around them. The eld woman watched the newly joined couple across from her, finding great joy in seeing two of her dearest friends whole and happy.

She looked down from the smiling faces of the Goblin King and his new bride to the young boy who lay sleeping in her lap. The boy who had been stolen away to faerie, now returned. The one whom she had agreed to take in and care for. She gently stroked her hand over his soft golden hair.

"His life will not be easy, standing between two worlds as he does," she said, a niggle of doubt worming its way into her heart. "And I am an old woman. It has been a long time since I cared for a child. I hope I remember how." She felt the truth of those words now more than she ever had, or at least more than she had in a very long time.

"*Pfft!*"

She turned her head and looked over at the phooka stretched out on the ground next to her.

"You are not so old. And it has not been that long..." Hoax said, smiling winsomely up at her. "A few centuries at the most."

She sighed with fond exasperation. "Only you would say such a ridiculous thing."

Lumina surprised her then, asking about the life she had lived before she had come to stay in the house at the wood's edge, when she had still lived among mortals. It was odd to think of those times. Just how old had she been when they had chased her from her village? She found that she wasn't sure of her answer.

"It was so long ago, I am not sure I remember," she admitted. "Forty, perhaps, not yet fifty, surely. At that time, it was quite a venerable age, though certainly nothing compared to the age I am now."

"Which is nothing to the age I am, since mine even rivals Lorne's by a goodly amount," the still grinning phooka quipped, the mischief in his eyes daring her to refute his statement.

"As great as all that," she said. "Then perhaps I should not trouble you to carry us home. I am not sure such ancient bones could hold us."

He was up on his feet in a thrice.

"Then allow me to disprove your theory," he said, sweeping her a mocking bow, "and prove to you once again that such things mean nothing at all."

She couldn't help but laugh. After all, what would he know about 'such things', having not a mortal bone in his body? Taking her leave of the happy couple, she allowed him to carry her away into the night, the boy tucked safely in front of her.

He took them straight home to the house at the wood's edge, with nary a stray from the path. A mighty feat for the phooka, she was sure. Right up to the garden gate he went, and before she could think to slide down, he was standing there in front of her, on two legs now instead of the four he had been on just a heartbeat ago. His strong arms held the boy's legs securely around his waist, while the boy's head rested quietly on his shoulder. She found herself on her own two feet as well, pressed up close to the goblin's back with the boy sleeping between them. The pony ears sticking up from the phooka's black hair twitched as he turned one green eye back over his shoulder to look at her.

"When you have a mind, could you open the gate? It seems my hands are a touch full."

She walked around him and did as he asked, casting a scowl in his direction, which he met with a smile.

Hoax brought the sleeping boy all the way through the house, past the cold hearth, to the bedroom just beyond where she had him put the boy into her own bed. She tucked the child in and stood there watching as he drifted off into true sleep.

The wind outside seemed filled with soft lamentations as it blew past. Whispered portents that sent a shiver down her back and made her wonder if even now the washer women were at the water's edge, washing her burial shroud. Or was that merely a flight of fancy brought on by her returned mortality?

The boy whimpered a little, and she reached down to stroke his hair. It was such a sad sound, one much like another she had heard recently. A picture of the cursed queen as a white hind flashed through her mind. The graceful doe, white as a hawthorn in flower, leaping away as she tried to flee from the mortal heart that now beat in her chest. The eld woman shivered again, remembering the sound the white hind had made, a cry filled with infinite hopelessness and despair. And despite their old enmity, the eld woman felt a moment's pity for the creature who was once the Fairy Queen.

A warm hand settled on her shoulder chasing the cold away. The forgotten phooka's green, green eyes shone bright as they smiled at her from the darkness. "Why yes of course, I would love some tea."

CHAPTER 1

A Summer Crown
for Winter's Head

Hoarfrost had turned the trees around them into a forest of spun glass. The eld woman made her way through the ebony trunks, stopping every few steps to cut evergreen and holly boughs. She tossed them over her shoulder into the large basket she was carrying on her back, to be woven later into garlands for the winter solstice.

Glancing around, she saw the boy, Thom, walking just a little way aways. The silver cat followed beside him on little prancing feet, as they crossed over the frost-covered ground towards her. The boy's eyes were bright as he looked at the spot where she stood. But she knew it was not her that he saw; perhaps he was watching the sylphs as they danced through the glittering wood around them. Or perhaps, it was an entirely different wood that he saw, one where crystal trees grew, and the queen of fairies ruled. Or had once ruled, as it was.

His absent gaze did not stop her from smiling at him anyway and speaking to him even though she knew he would not answer. She did not take his silence personally. In the past month, since he had come to live with her, she had taken up the habit of explaining what she was doing and why, even though it seemed as if his attention was elsewhere. She understood what it was like to see what others could not, and how difficult it could be to walk in that space between two worlds. Unfortunately, she suspected that for Thom it was the mortal realm which appeared as if it were a dream, and the hidden one that was his reality.

They came to a small dell where the air felt warmer. She stopped, staring at the patches of color around her. The flowers, in their confusion, had sprung up from the ground despite the sparkling frost, making themselves into a summer crown for winter's icy head. Had it been early spring, she would have thought nothing of it, but it was only just midwinter. She frowned. She could not say why, but a deep feeling of unease whispered through her.

A warm hand slipped into hers, and she was surprised to find Thom standing next to her. He was looking down at the flowers as well, his brow furrowed in the same way she suspected hers was. She smiled at the top of his head.

"A few more and we will be finished," she told him, squeezing his hand.

She continued on with her gathering, but it was not long after that she turned them towards home. Thom held her hand the whole way back, while the silver cat, declaring his paws half frozen, rode in the basket atop the evergreens.

That afternoon found her standing at the table, the ever-greens she had gathered earlier stretched out before her like a miniature forest. The warmth of the hearth was at her back as she deftly wove the fragrant greens into garlands, wrapping them in red thread and stringing them with silver and brass bells. She watched the snow blow past as she went about her task; the window's multi-hued panes making a kaleidoscope of the flurries as they swirled by.

In only a few hours, the weather had turned bitter. The snow, which was at best only a light dusting at this time a year, was even now piling up into tall drifts. Usually, she did not mind being snowed in, enjoying the hush of the world outside as the snow blanketed the house. As long as the water butt and pantry were full, there was little need for her to go much further than the spring cellar door. But this year was different.

Glancing back over her shoulder, she found Thom sitting on the hearth rug watching the fire, the silver cat curled up next to him was fast asleep. Checking on the boy was something else she found herself doing often now. An increasingly familiar weight settled on her shoulders even as she looked at him fondly.

She had not had a name for that feeling of heaviness the first time she felt it, but she did now. Strangely enough, it was loneliness. The loneliness of caring for Thom on her own, and the uncertainty of what the years ahead would bring for him. And for herself as well, if she were honest. It was a foolish feeling perhaps, but she felt it all the same.

Once the garlands were done, she set about hanging them above the windows. The sharp piney scent of them tickled her nose as the bells strung throughout winked merrily back at her in the firelight.

She had just finished hanging the last one when there was a sharp tap, tap, tapping at her window. Opening it, she found a snow-covered raven perched on the sill. He wasted no time in shaking off his feathers and hopping inside.

"*Fah!* My wings are nearly frozen," the phooka declared, gliding from the table to a spot on the floor, closer to the hearth.

"What did you expect, flying out in such weather?" she asked, closing the window behind him.

"*Tch!* Cold-hearted! That's what you are. Suddenly, the weather outside seems balmy," the phooka said, shedding his feathers and holding his hands out to the fire. "And here I am, having braved the elements, riding on the very back of the Northwind no less, all the way here just to tell you..."

There was a knocking at the door.

"...to expect visitors," she finished his sentence for him as she made her way towards it.

"Just so," he grinned.

Answering the knock, she found a golden-eyed Lumina standing there smiling at her, snowflakes strewn through her hair like a string of stars in a blue evening sky. The sprite's arms were full of snow-dusted bundles which she began to hand to Hoax, who appeared as by magic from inside the cottage.

Lumina turned around to the pale stag standing behind her, unloading the last of the bundles from his back before stepping inside. The White Stag, now relieved of his burdens, followed in on his bride's heels, changing to his more human seeming as he ducked his antlered head to cross the threshold.

"Welcome," the eld woman said, kissing first Lumina, then Lorne on the cheek as they moved past her. "What is all this?"

"We've come to spend the solstice with you," Lorne said, walking over to where the various bundles had been piled. "And we brought gifts."

He began unwrapping them one by one. The first held a warm coat for Thom. The ones that followed were filled with shirts and trousers and a sturdy pair of shoes, all just the right size for the boy.

There was also a great deal of food to be had: wheels of cheese, loaves of bread, a cold ham, and small bags stuffed with sugared fruits and nuts. There was even a tightly tied basket of cranberries sitting off to one side, which she immediately set Thom to stringing.

Leaving them to the unwrapping, she pulled on her old shawl and made her way through the narrow door that would take her to the spring cellar. Just as she had hoped, there was still a jug of cider left from the batch she had made out of last season's apples. They had been gathered from the progeny of the old apple tree, and though they did not contain the same virtue of immortality as their parent, they were tasty and made excellent cider.

When she returned, she found there was barely room on the table for the jug she was carrying, so full of food was it. Which was fine because the cider was soon in a pot, set high over the fire to warm, spices from her dwindling stores simmering serenely atop the golden liquid.

They ate and laughed while they hung strings of cranberries, taking care to light the candles she had waiting in the windows, so that their warm glow would shine out into the darkness beyond.

She tucked Thom into bed just around midnight. The silver cat followed along, claiming that his hearth rug was too crowded. Which was true, for the rest of her guests were all sitting together on the floor in front of the fire, content in each other's company, sipping mulled cider as they reminisced about the passing year.

And what a year it had been! It had seen one of her oldest friends, and her newest, find their happiness in each other. It saw herself give up a gift beyond price when she gave the oldest tree's last apple to Lumina. Which she did knowing full well that by doing so, she would once again age as any mortal would, for a time at least. And it brought her Thom, and with him, the changing of her whole world.

The shushing snow outside and warmth of the fire in front of them conspired to lull everyone into a dreamy contentment. Lumina and Lorne lay to one side of the hearth, heads pillowed on each other's hips, and she could not help but smile softly at the sight. Perhaps it should have seemed odd to have such beautiful, otherworldly creatures tangled together like two kittens asleep on her hearth rug, but it didn't. Seeing their happiness had chased away the loneliness of before, reminding her of when she was young. Of long nights just like this one, spent in front of a fire, keeping warm with friends or lovers.

She felt a soft weight settle across her back. The phooka's chin came to rest on her shoulder, his breath warm on her cheek as he spoke low next to her ear.

"Do you wish that for yourself?" he whispered, in a voice made for secrets.

"What would make you ask something so foolish?" she retorted softly.

"Am I asking something foolish?"

How to explain the different aspects of love to a creature such as the one sitting next to her?

"Yes, you are. And if you understood the human heart, you would know how foolish a question it was," she replied.

"Perhaps, and perhaps the question I am asking is not the one you are answering," he suggested, smoothing his hands over her shoulders as he moved away.

He had left something behind. Her fingers, reaching up, brushed across fabric thick and luxuriant. Drawing it closer, she saw that it was a lovely green shawl, beautifully woven. The silken threads beneath her fingertips were cottony and soft, and unlike anything she had seen before.

"I don't see why Thom should be the only one to receive gifts," he said, wrapping the shawl more securely around her shoulders. "A gift freely given. To keep you warm, and to give me a soft place to rest my weary head," he finished, laying his head on her shoulder, daring her to admonish him.

She sighed in defeat and fond exasperation, allowing him to stay where he was. Resting her own cheek against the top of his head, she watched as the salamanders danced in the fire. The furry tip of Hoax's ear twitching ever-so-softly against her lips with each out-going breath.

"Do you want to see something wondrous?" a voice whispered quietly in her ear, waking her from sleep.

She opened her eyes to find herself looking up into Hoax's face, her head now lying comfortably in his lap. He gestured for her to stand, so she did, wincing as her stiff muscles complained. Hoax took her hand and led her to the window nearest the hearth, its glass panes, traced in frost, hid the world outside behind icy lace. He undid the latch, opening it just a crack so that they might see out.

The night was clear now, sharp-edged, and brilliantly cold. Just beyond the linden tree she could see two figures dancing out on the snow.

Their feet left no prints to mark their passage. No music guided their steps, or at least no music that she could hear, yet they moved with sureness and grace. The moon was caught up in his silver antlers and the stars tangled themselves in her hair. With each sway and turn the world was made right around them. Spring was in every touch they shared, and autumn in every kiss. Every parting brought with it winter and every return summer. Their dance was eternal, and in that infinite moment, the music of the world revealed itself. It was a song not meant for mortal ears, though they themselves were a part of it. The endlessness of eternity filled her mind as she understood truths she knew she would not remember. She was but a mortal being, and her heart ached as she watched the dancers. They were as stars in the sky, pure and beautiful and so very far above her.

A warm hand cupped her cheek, wiping away tears she had not even known were there.

"This is not at all what I intended." And for once the phooka's face was serious. "Forgive me, sweet witch; I did not think. Humble beings such as you and I are not meant for such lofty things."

"Such lofty things?" she repeated, her ire growing unreasonably. "Is that what you think I wish for? Only a fool tries to hold the sun. I, for one, would much rather bask in its warmth."

"Would you? I thought you loved him once."

"I do still," she admitted. "But not as I think you mean it."

"You sacrificed half your sight for him," the phooka pointed out.

She had given up much more than that to see Lorne happy and whole, but she had no desire to bring the phooka's attention to that.

"And when he was blind, you were his eyes for a century or more. Though you were no more obligated to do so than I was," she retorted, annoyed at his interrogation, yet at the same time feeling perversely grateful for it. "You will admit there are those who are deserving of such kindnesses. Ones like your king and his bride, who do for others with no thought of gain for themselves."

"I will wholeheartedly admit it," he said, closing the window. The dancers disappeared from her sight behind the frost-laced glass. "But your answer is really no answer at all."

"It is as plain an answer as you could ask for, and certainly plainer than any one you have ever given."

"That may be, but I think I need it to be even plainer."

"Even plainer?" she scoffed. "How can I be any plainer than 'I love him still'? Is it the 'still' or the 'love' that I need to make plainer?"

"Oh 'love', definitely 'love'. I think everyone could stand to have that made plainer!" he laughed softly. "And I am curious to know what you meant when you said, 'not as I think you mean it'."

"I am not going to try to explain the different aspects of love to a twisty-tongued creature such as you," she said, voicing her thoughts from earlier. "You would get too much pleasure out of spinning my words on their heads."

"Explanations of love should set your head spinning," he nodded sagely, but the twinkle in his eye told her he was taking great delight in teasing her.

"*Ach!* You make me tired," she said.

"I could if you would only let me!"

"Enough, you ridiculous goblin," she said with familiar exasperation.

Hoax held his tongue, smiling at her in much the same way as the silver cat did when he happened upon an unattended crock of cream. She eyed him suspiciously, wondering what mischief he was up to.

There was a shifting in the world around her, a turning of the tide. Though the darkness still held sway, the longest night was over. The old year was passing, and soon the sun would rise, bringing with it a new year and new beginnings.

CHAPTER 2

On the Breath
of the Storm

The eld woman stood in her doorway, watching the spring storm roll down off the moors. The black clouds advanced like a conquering army across the brilliant evening sky.

She could see a figure moving just ahead of it, a dark horse dancing on the breath of the storm. The wind ringing madly through the hedge bells heralded his arrival. He came right up through her garden gate, proud neck arched and hooves flashing as he met her at the door, his green eyes aglow like ghost lights in a graveyard.

"Come for a ride with me," he coaxed, nodding his fine pony head at her rakishly. "You could not ask for a finer evening! We can dance in the raindrops until we are soaked through and through, then amuse ourselves getting dry again."

"I am not letting you take me for a ride in the rain, Hoax," she chided, shaking her head at the phooka's nonsense. "Come in and be quick about it, before you get soaked 'through and through'. No need for you to drip water all across my floor."

"As my lady commands," he said as lightning flashed in the darkness, revealing the changed phooka standing in front of her. Green eyes now glinted at her from a handsome youth's face stretched wide with a mischievous smile.

Sighing at his foolishness, she headed back into the house, knowing he would follow at her heels. She heard the door closing behind her as she made her way to the table where Thom sat staring into the fire, smiling at the salamanders that danced there.

"Dinner will be ready in just a moment," she said, reaching out to stroke the boy's thick golden hair as she walked past him towards where dinner sat simmering on the hearth.

Giving the pot a stir, she turned to find the table's only other chair occupied by a dark-haired scoundrel who was watching her with pitiful eyes and a mournful expression.

Resigning herself to the inevitable, she pulled an extra bowl and cup down from the shelf and placed it on the table. Next came the bread, which she put out on the board before filling the bowls from the pot hanging in the hearth. Having finished that, she started looking around for another place to sit, since the only two seats at the table were occupied. Hoax winked at her and patted his knee, laughing merrily when she scowled back at him. Still chuckling, he stood, offering her the chair he had been sitting on, which was rightly hers to begin with. He pulled a stool from where it sat near the door, placing it at the head of the table between herself and Thom.

The wind sang through the crack under the door and the rain began pelting the glass as they sat down to eat. She raised her spoon to her lips, watching as the phooka tapped the back of the boy's hand with one blunt-nailed finger. The boy turned his gaze towards him; reaching out he stroked the furry tips of the pony ears that peeked up through the phooka's wild black hair. Hoax, showing infinite patience, only lifted the spoon from his own bowl. He brought it up to his mouth, holding onto the boy's gaze as he did so. The boy followed his example, taking up his own spoon and slowly eating until all his dinner was gone. She was grateful for that. It was not always easy to get Thom to eat. Not surprising she supposed, mortal food having little to offer when compared to the delicacies of the Fairy Queen's court. Except for the ability to sustain life, of course. In that, the fairies' food, like many other things from Underhill, held only empty promises.

After everyone had finished, she gathered up the dishes and set about scouring them clean. Outside the thunder grumbled and growled as the wind whistled by. The sylphs riding on its back shrieked gleefully, taking great delight in tapping on her windows as they raced past.

She had not expected Hoax to stay much after dinner was done, but to her surprise he did. He lounged on the hearth rug, seemingly content to sit there and watch as Thom drew designs in the ashes by the fire.

Even as the hour grew later, the phooka still showed no signs of leaving. So she went about her business, adding oats and dried fruit to a pot, covering them with water and placing it on the hearth, not too close to the fire, so that it would be ready for the morning. That done, she took herself and the boy off to the other room to get ready for sleep.

She stood him in front of the wash basin that was in a corner of the room, on a table opposite the bed. Pouring water warmed earlier into it, she handed him a cloth and instructed him to wash.

He did as she asked while she pulled out the feather ticking she kept in a chest at the end of the bed. Setting it aside, she changed into her night rail, laying her dress out across the top of the chest so that it was ready for the next day. Reminding Thom to continue washing every time she noticed his attention drift, his eyes staring out of the window in front of where the basin sat.

When he finally finished, she tucked him into her bed. Then gathering up her brush, a ribbon and the feather ticking, she wished Thom a good night and left.

The room she returned to was dark, save for the light coming from the fire. She laid her bedding out in front of the hearth, sinking down on it gratefully once it was in place. She began to brush and braid her hair, listening as the storm continued unabated outside.

"Is this where you've been sleeping since the boy arrived?" Hoax's voice asked. Turning she found him stretched out on the floor behind her, hands beneath his head.

"Where else would I sleep? The boy needs the bed more than I do," she stated, although her stiff joints begged to differ.

"I can well imagine you change your mind when the fire burns low. But, there is no need for you to sleep cold on the hearth tonight," he assured her. "For here I am, perfect for curling up with. And should you need a bit of comfort in the middle of the night, you can always reach over and rub my belly."

"Should *I* need a bit of comfort?" she said dryly.

"Well, it would certainly comfort me," he replied drolly, stretching out to his full length, before turning on his side to face her. The winsome eyes looking back at her now in the face of a great black hound.

The impertinent thing stood up and nosed his way onto the bedding despite her protests, laying down next to her with a sigh. She gave up and lay down also, turning her back to the phooka, exasperating creature that he was. Still, his gentle breathing seemed to lift a weight from her shoulders, and the heat coming from him eased the aches in her body better than the fire she lay in front of. Aches that were more than they should be because of the usual lack of them. Feeling more at ease than she had in a while, she slid down into sleep.

She dreamt of Mayings long past, of garlands and flowered crowns, and the warm kiss of the spring sun on her skin. Dreams of dancing in the moonlight with a sweet tune in her ears and sweeter kisses on her lips. Teasing promises whispered in the dark woke a longing for such things that had never truly been hers. The hypnotic feel of silken skin beneath her fingers as she ran her hands across it…

Her eyes drifted open, finding that the fire had burned down very low; it would go out if she did not put a log on it soon. But she could not seem to bring herself to move, comfortable as she was, her hand stroking along the warm silken flank next to her. A flank that was no longer covered in fur.

She sat up, wincing softly as she did so. Moving carefully, she shifted to her knees slowly in the hopes of not waking the goblin man who was currently taking up half her bed. Her joints protested loudly against the chill that had settled in the house, now that she was away from the phooka's warmth. A soft groan hummed in her throat as she leaned over to add a log to the fire.

Hoax had not moved. Assuming him still asleep, she settled back down into his warmth.

"Tell me, eld woman, just how heavily does your mortal blood weigh on you, now that you do not have old man apple's gift to hold it back?" His soft question from the darkness beside her proved her earlier assumption a lie.

"Go to sleep, you troublesome creature," was all the answer she gave him, having no desire to discuss such things in the middle of the night.

"You first, dearheart."

Her eyelids grew heavy with his words, sleep stealing up on soft feet to claim her.

When she woke the next morning, she was alone on her bedding. The phooka had not left a single dog hair behind on the ticking for her to be annoyed about. That in and of itself, she found extremely annoying.

Though if she were honest with herself, she had slept better last night then in all the time since Thom had come to live with her, this past Hollentide. Not that she would ever admit such a thing to the one responsible for it.

She built up the fire and wrapped her shawl tight about her, before stealing out the door, kettle in hand.

The air was crisp and clean from the storm that had come through the night before. Puddles reflecting the sky above lay scattered like silver coins across the garden. The ground squished wetly beneath her feet as she walked around to where the spring's cold water fell gently from a stone spout.

Normally she reveled in such mornings, enjoying the quiet that often came when a chill was in the air. But her time was no longer her own, and she felt an urgency to return indoors, knowing there were things that needed doing. A sharp feeling of resentment stabbed at her. It was natural to chaff under a yoke of obligation, even one you had chosen for yourself. So she allowed herself to feel annoyance for just a moment, before releasing it out into the still morning to burn up like mist in the rising sun.

She returned indoors, putting the kettle on to heat and moving yesterday's pot of porridge closer to the fire. Bending over, she gathered up the bedding from where it lay in front of the hearth, her bones protesting as she did so. She did feel old, damn the phooka's eyes for noticing.

Her arms filled with the feather ticking, she made her way back into the bedroom, thinking to find Thom still in bed. Instead, she found him up and already dressed looking out of the same window he had been the night before. He did not look at her when she came in, and she had not expected him to. She greeted him nonetheless.

"Good morning…" she started to say then blinked, taking notice of a fairly large change in the room.

A second bed to be exact, with a familiar silver cat stretched out across its thick coverlet.

"Good morning," he said, stretching his toes and blinking at her. "Your new bed is very comfortable." He jumped down, busking her legs as he walked past. "Better if you tried it later through. No need to put off breakfast."

She continued on her trek, ignoring him in favor of putting the bedding back in the chest she had taken it from the night before.

"Thom," she said, touching the boy's shoulder as she walked past. "Please go sit at the table. I'll be out in a moment to get your breakfast."

The boy did not acknowledge that he had heard her but he did do as she instructed. She finished putting away the bedding she was holding and followed him out.

Thom sat at the table, as she had asked, while she spooned the porridge from the pot. She poured a little cream over the top before placing the bowl in front of him. A small bowl of cream also went in front of the silver cat who had been surprisingly patient as he waited. Then, filling a pitcher with warm water, she headed back into the room to perform her morning ablutions.

It was peaceful this early in the day. The windows were open, and the sunlight poured through them, pooling onto the floor in neat golden squares. Closing the door, she carried the pitcher over to the washstand, and set it down next to a waiting basin. A generous portion of rosewater went into the basin first and the warm water from the pitcher followed soon after. Little fragrant ghosts billowed up from the surface as she untied her night rail and let it fall to her feet. Stepping from the pile of cloth, she picked it up and lay it out on the chest near her, next to the skirts she had placed there the night before.

Naked, she began to wash. The honeyed sun fell around her, warming her skin despite the chill in the air. She dipped a soft cloth in the water and gently began to wipe away the sweat leftover from sleep. Goosebumps flashed along her skin as whispers of last night's dream rose up with the sweet-scented steam. She had to admit, even if only to herself, that she had enjoyed the warmth of a body lying next to hers in the dark. Though the innocence of her shared bed from the night before was nothing like the long-forgotten memories that it had conjured. She was sure that if the phooka were ever to find out, there would be no end to her hearing about it.

The remembrances of her youth gave way to the realities of the present as she dried herself. Noticing for the first time in a long while the changes the passing years had wrought to her body. Her skin, though still healthy, lacked the firmness it once had. And her hair hanging loose as it was made it easy to see the thick streaks of silver running through it. She began to dress, shaking her head and wondering when it was that she had become such a vain creature.

She pulled on a clean shift. Over the top of that went the skirts she had laid out on the trunk and over top of it all went the brown caraco.

As she was fastening up the front, her gaze drifted over to the new bed, with its green coverlet. She went to stand at the foot of it, casting a gimlet eye over the thing while she brushed and rebraided her hair. She had a strong feeling that this was the phooka's doing and wondered what mischief he was about. Friends they may be, but goblin gifts were still goblin gifts and they rarely came for free.

An empty table greeted her when she stepped from the room. She was alone in the house with no sign of Thom or the silver cat anywhere. Her heart fluttered like a caged bird in her chest as a cold weight settled low in her belly. Grabbing her shawl, she quickly headed out the door in the hopes of catching up to him.

When she had begun her search, it was with the idea that she would find her wayward charge in short order. However now, with over two hours having past, all her reason had fled, consumed entirely by panic and dread. She reasoned that it was unlikely any of the Hidden Folk would harm Thom. He was in her care after all, and thus under the protection of the Goblin King, but the wood still held other dangers of a more common nature. And what if he had gotten himself lost? What if she was mistaken in where she thought he was going?

She consoled herself with the fact that the silver cat was most likely with him, only to have her doubt remind her that she did not know that to be true either.

It was nearly another hour before a familiar black raven came winging up to land on her shoulder.

"If you've lost something, I think I've found it," he said, grooming a strand of hair away from her ear.

Relief and irritation swept through her in equal measure, the unfortunate phooka bearing the brunt of the latter.

"If you know where he is then carry me to him instead of making an old woman work so hard," she admonished him. "I am nearly out of breath!" Which was sadly true.

"Old woman," Hoax scoffed. "That phrase is on your lips often of late. Do you say it to convince me or yourself? As for being out of breath... well if I was one who was inclined to more *earthy* thoughts, I am sure I would have a thing or two to say about being breathless."

"You infuriating creature! If you do not wish me to pluck you bald, you will change and give me a ride," she panted, her anger getting the better of her.

The phooka chuckled in her ear, undaunted by her threats. "Well, when you ask so sweetly, how can I say nay?"

He launched himself from her shoulder, and between one step and the next, was standing on the path in front of her, shaking his riotous mane in laughter. But she was in no mood to appreciate his pun. She climbed onto his back as quickly as she could. As soon as she was settled, he was away, moving at such a pace that the wind itself could not have caught them had it tried.

It was no time at all before they arrived at the stream that had once served as the boundary between the goblin's wood and those lands belonging to the Fairy Queen. The crossing, which they would have normally used, was flooded, but there standing at its edge was Thom, his unshod toes in the icy water as though he thought to cross anyway. The silver cat was sitting not far away, eyeing the frothing water with distrust.

"Thom," she called out as she slid from Hoax's back. The calm, steady sound of her voice belied the emotions twisting around inside her. Thom did not turn his head to look, but she knew he was listening. "I was worried," she said, walking up to stand beside him.

He continued looking in the direction of the meadow and the familiar glade just beyond it. She followed his gaze, noticing that the lake stretched unusually far beyond its banks. The still waters reflected the sky above, so that the drowned meadow's flowers looked as though they were pushing their way up through the clouds themselves. It seemed that Spring was showing itself to be just as muddled as this past Winter had been.

"Are you looking for something?" She asked the question not really expecting him to answer, but surprisingly he did just that.

"She is not here," he said, with a voice like an apathetic angel.

"The Blue-Rose Woman?" she asked. It was a name he often used when talking about Lumina. Which in a way made perfect sense, given that was exactly what Lumina had been on the day of her wedding, and it was Thom who had planted her as a seed in the very same meadow over which he now looked.

"No," was all he said, turning back instead towards the goblins' wood without further explanation.

"Well then, since what you were looking for isn't here, we might as well look somewhere else," suggested Hoax, appearing as a hound at the boy's side. "And as we look, we can let the 'old woman' following us load our pockets with the stuff she finds."

"No pockets," said the boy, taking hold of the hound's ruff.

"Why you're right, I don't have any pockets! I guess we'll have to use your pockets then," said the phooka, looking back and winking at her with one glowing green eye. He led the boy off into the wood. Shaking her head, she set off after them. She should have known there would be no straight path home if she were to follow a phooka.

The way they took back through the wood was indeed a meandering one. Over hills and through dells they went, and along little streams where the willows happily grew. It was mid-afternoon by the time they returned to the house at the edge of the wood, their pockets full of violets and their arms full of willow wands.

Again, the phooka surprised her by staying, eating a late lunch at the table with them just as he had eaten dinner the night before. Thom sat watching him all the while, eating as the phooka ate until the plate in front of him was empty.

The day had turned out very fine. The clouds above sailed like great white galleons across a sea of pastoral blue. They had made their way out into the garden after lunch. Thom lay on his back in a bed of clover, while the eld woman, tired from the day's adventures, sat on an old stone seat beneath the linden tree. The silver cat lay purring in her lap. The phooka had stretched himself out on the ground facing her, hands behind his black-haired head. His feet were propped up comfortably on the seat beside her knee. She could feel his green eyes watching her even as she contemplated the boy who lay staring up at the sky.

"You worry about him?" he asked her after a while.

"I do," she admitted.

"Why?"

How was she to explain all the vague, nameless worries that came with caring for another mortal being, or for that matter, the worries that came with just being mortal. Worries she herself had left behind long ago until recent events had brought them back down on her shoulders a hundred-fold.

"With your brow furrowed like that you look like there is a storm brewing on your forehead," said Hoax, smiling unrepentantly when she turned her sharp gaze on him. "Have you lost the boy so many times before, then?" he asked.

"I have not 'lost' the boy before," she said, frowning at him. "But I did find him outside more than once this winter, barefoot in the snow."

"So, it is a burden," Hoax said.

"No, and yes," she admitted quietly, compelled to honesty by the weight she felt on her shoulders. "He does not make trouble for trouble's sake, but he barely sees the mortal world at all, much less the dangers of it. Which means that I must always keep watch." Her confession tasted bitter on her tongue even as she said it.

"There was no reason for you to watch alone," Hoax pointed out.

"And who would you have me ask?"

"I see a likely candidate in front of you," said the silver cat stretching first one foot then the other as he left her lap, jumping down to go sit next to the phooka. "After all, what else is he doing?"

"Lazing about the same as you, I'm sure," she said. The silver cat ignored her in favor of washing his ears.

"He is right you know," the phooka said from where he lay, covered in shadowy lace cast by the linden tree's still-bare branches. "My king has little need for me now that he has found his heart again. So, I am free to help as you need me."

She scoffed. "But would your help be free?"

"As free as you want it to be," he said, smiling innocently up at her with mischief-filled eyes.

"See, my suggestion is perfect," said the silver cat, cleaning his shoulder unconcernedly.

"And where would you sleep?" she asked the phooka.

"On your pillow or at your feet, whichever you prefer," he replied, his smile growing wider.

The eld woman's lips quirked up despite themselves. What was she getting herself into? "Well, if you are going to stay here, you might as well start making yourself useful."

The evening wind felt unusually warm for early spring as they walked back from the furthest corner of the garden where the beehives stood. The nights might have been cool enough to make her joints ache, but the days were warm enough to trick her both garden and the bees into thinking summer was nearly upon them. So even though it was too early in the year for it, the hives were already stuffed full of honey.

"See I told you I would be useful," Hoax said, quite obviously pleased with himself.

She couldn't argue on that account as she was currently carrying a bucket filled with the sticky fruits of their labor, with not a single sting for her trouble. Had she known having a silver-tongued phooka around would make honey harvesting so easy, she would have conscripted him for it long ago.

Thom was walking in front of them, the long light of the setting sun shining brightly in his golden hair. Little breezes raced through the garden causing the bells to ring gently in the hedges around them. She hoped the boy was happy here, though his tendency to wander wreaked havoc on her peace of mind. She did not know what it was about the sight in front of her, but it started her thinking about ways she could find Thom when the need arose; a need she feared would only arise more and more frequently. A charm, or perhaps a binding, something that could allow him to find her as well, should he need to.

She thought about it all through dinner, the idea taking shape as she ate. Later as she was brushing Thom's hair, she plucked a few golden strands from the boy's head. Hoax noticed of course but he kept his questions to himself, only offering to tuck Thom into bed for her.

While he was doing so, she began laying out what she would need on the hearthstones, careful to keep them well away from the flames. She could have laid everything out on the larger table just behind her, or even the smaller one near her wing chair, where the oil lamp sat. But for this, it was important that the magic she did be connected to hearth and home. So, she settled on a cushion in front of the fire, adding the strands of Thom's hair to the other things that waited there.

"Are you making a charm?" the phooka asked, startling her a bit as he leaned over her shoulder to see what she was about.

"If the boy insists on setting off on his own, then I think it best," she replied, carefully cutting thin strips from the deerskin in front of her.

"What are they meant to do?"

"They will bind us together, in a way, letting each of us know where the other is," she explained, not stopping in her industry.

The phooka came around to sit on the hearth rug close to her. "Then I think it best if you were to make me one as well."

"Do you?" she said, amused. "I would think that such a binding would be uncomfortable for the likes of you."

"If you think that, then you have not been paying attention," he admonished her. "What else have I been but bound for these past four centuries."

"It didn't seem as though you were," she commented. "But if that was so, then I would think it all the more reason you would not wish to be again."

"There are many things that bind us and many ways to be bound. And not all of them are unwelcome," he pointed out. "So, tell me, what do you need, my blood… my love… my name…"

"Don't offer such things so carelessly!" she snapped, a shiver running through her at the thought of him gifting such power to someone.

"Why? Are you afraid I would give them to you?" His ever-growing grin pinned her with his question.

"I do think you might, just for the sheer mischief of it!" she declared, finding herself uneasy. "No, I only need to pluck a few hairs from your head."

"Then pluck away!" he said, moving nearer so she could reach more easily.

"Impossible goblin," she huffed as she leaned forward, sliding her hands into his hair.

A surprising thought came to her then. For all the centuries she had known the phooka, she could not think of a time when she had so deliberately reached out to touch him when his shape was that of a man's. For some reason, she found that knowledge unsettling as the cool strands of his hair glided over her fingers. Smoother than any silk, they slipped through her hands, and try as she might, she could not seem to keep hold of any of them.

"You will have to be more determined if you are to catch them," he said, chuckling low as he bent his head further for her.

"Behave," she told him, ignoring the way his voice slid over her skin as she leaned even closer. Her fingers gently running through his hair until they met each other at the very back of his head where she was finally able to pluck three obsidian strands. "So much trouble," she said, turning her head to find his smiling face much closer than she expected. For a moment, her breath stilled. The world seemed to contract, vanishing until the island of soft firelight around them was all that remained.

"My turn, I believe," he breathed.

She felt a soft tug on her braid from where it had fallen into his lap. Slowly she sat back, unsure of the strange air between them as he began to undo her braid. She let him, unmoving, as he carefully unwound the long plait, his movements achingly slow as he gently combed his fingers through her hair. She was suddenly conscious of every silver strand, of every line in her face. Even the sightless orb that was her left eye abruptly became a thing of which she was vividly aware. All the while he watched her knowingly with his green, green eyes.

She knew him to be older than herself by many, many centuries. But for all appearances, he was a man still fresh in his youth, smooth-skinned and leanly muscled. His body fully grown, but lacking the bulk of maturity. A maturity he would never see because he was not a mortal man at all.

The comfortable familiarity of their long friendship shifted like sand beneath her as, for the first time, she saw him as a man. A well-made goblin man, with a generous smiling mouth and eyes full of mischievous promise. And there she sat, world-worn and mortal, feeling the differences between them as she never had before.

He snorted softly at her.

"Close your eyes," he said, tenderly running his fingertips over her eyelids. "They deceive you too easily. As the eyes of all mortals do." But at that moment it was not her eyes she was worried about.

The darkness afforded a timelessness to the gentle tug and pull as he continued to comb his fingers through her hair. The endless moment dissolved as she thought she felt the ghost of a kiss brush her lips.

Her eyes snapped open, only to find the phooka sitting back on his heels. He was much further away than she had expected, making her doubt for a moment the feeling that lingered on her lips. But the oh-so-innocent smile on his face as he happily wove the three strands of her hair between his fingers lendt itself more to confirming her suspicions than to allaying them.

She decided not to say anything, mostly because she felt that he was expecting her to have something to say. Instead, she silently took the strands of hair from him, coiling them together with the others in a swirl of silver, gold and inky black before setting them to the side.

The silence held between them. Hoax quietly watched as she spun flax and nettle into thread, twisting the strands of hair in as she twined the fibers together. A bowl of water sat on the floor at her elbow, the scent of rosemary rising up from it every time she dipped her fingers in to wet them while she spun.

Midnight came and went before everything was finally ready. The moon shone brightly through the window's jewel-tone glass as she drew her thread across the beeswax. Sitting in the firelight with her bone awl and silver needle, she hummed softly as she carefully worked the thread through the soft leather, a pattern slowly forming in its wake. She continued working through the night though her eyes ached, so intent on her task, she barely noticed when the still silent phooka changed into a hound, making a backrest of himself for her to lean against.

When dawn came, the three bands lay done. Every inch was covered with a pattern of turnsole flowers and twining morning glory vines. Small clapperless bells hung at each point where a trumpet-shaped flower would have bloomed.

Her eyes felt gritty as she blinked in the growing light. Standing up, she went over to stir up the fire before going out to fill the kettle. She returned to find Hoax holding one of the bands, running his fingers along the stitching. Putting the kettle on to heat, she sat back down on the hearth rug across from where he was, taking note of the phooka's odd silence for the first time.

"Are you reconsidering?" she asked him.

"Are you?" he grinned at her impishly.

"It is not a thing to be entered into lightly," she counseled. "Such a thing cannot be easily broken."

"Indeed," he said, his smile widening. "Come then, let me bind you quick, before you come to your senses."

She huffed, holding her arm out to him, watching as he circled her wrist with the band and sewed the ends together tightly with red thread. Once he had finished, she took up one of the remaining bands and wrapped it around his wrist, taking the needle and thread from him with her other hand. She held his eyes as she did so, wondering again if such a creature was made to be bound so. His grin softened into a smile as he guided her hand down towards the waiting band. She took her time, sewing the seams as carefully and as tightly as he had hers. As she tied the final knot, a faint sound resonated through the room, floating on the air like wind chimes. She severed the remaining thread, setting it to the side.

Looking back up she noticed the phooka's ears twitch, his eyes wide with wonder and delight. Hopping to his feet, he scooped her up as easily as he would a child, spinning her round and round while she sputtered and spat at him like a cat. He only stopped when the noise they were making brought Thom and the silver cat out from the bedroom where they had still been sleeping.

They stared at her and the phooka with large blinking eyes still soft from sleep. The silver cat made his way over to the recently abandoned hearth rug, sniffing at the needle and thread that still lay there. Thom, however, came over to where they were standing. He was not looking at them, but at the bands around their wrists. He reached out, tracing his finger through the air between them as though running it along a thread that only he could see. He reached down, picking up the remaining band and wrapping it around his wrist. He held it out, his blue-green eyes looking directly into hers. He kept surprising her when she least expected. Smiling at him, she began carefully binding the ends together, just as she had done for the phooka.

CHAPTER 3

Portents and Ill Airs

It had rained again the night before, as it had most nights since the phooka had come to live with them. Often as not those wet nights had turned into wetter days, but that morning when she opened the door she was greeted by fine weather and a clear sky. The sylphs, who were amusing themselves by racing ripples across the puddles leftover from last night's storm, promised her that no more rain was forthcoming. So, she considered her fast emptying stores and came to the conclusion that now may be a good time to do a little restocking. Feeding and clothing herself had never taken much; feeding and clothing a growing boy was a different story.

Once everyone had eaten, she packed a barrow full of things with which she could trade and set off with Thom and the helpful phooka in tow. She left the safety of the goblins' wood behind, pushing the barrow along muddy, rutted lanes, checking over her shoulder frequently as was her habit now, to see Thom still following with the monstrous black hound walking at his side. Each time she did, the phooka gave her a lolling grin for her trouble.

No matter where they went, the land was flooded. Seed, newly sprouted, lay rotting in the drowned fields. She shook her head at the sight; this coming harvest would likely be a poor one.

As they passed by a break in the hedgerow, she heard someone hallo her. She stopped, lowering the barrow's handles to wave back at the farmer who was standing in the field just beyond.

"Fair morning to you good henwife! Or at least I have hopes that it will be fair," the farmer said from behind the handles of his mired plow. "The seasons seem to not be able to make up their minds this year."

"I have noticed that, as well," she agreed.

"If you have a mind to stop by, Ayla is up at the house. She would be glad to see you."

"I will then," she said, picking up the barrow's handles and continuing down the lane to where a short wall of stacked stone replaced the hedgerow.

The farmer did not ask about the boy walking with her, nor did he mention the black hound that followed at his side. But she noticed him watching them with interest as they turned onto the small lane that led up to the farmhouse.

The neatly kept little house stood only a short way from the road. It was not the same farmhouse as the one where Lumina first made her fateful decision to steal the goblin's tribute, but it was a close neighbor to it and the owners were in the habit of leaving a bowl of milk and bread with honey on the stoop just as the others had. A young girl and boy were in the yard, taking turns at the butter churn. The farmhouse door stood open and the eld woman could see the farmwife busily kneading bread on the kitchen table.

The hound headed over to where the children were working, Thom followed along with his hand on the hound's ruff. She paused for a moment, but Hoax seemed to have everything in hand so she left him to it. Pulling a basket from the barrow, she continued on into the house.

It had been a year or so since she had last visited, and she was happy to see the farmwife rosy-cheeked and healthy. It was a vast improvement from when last she had seen her, still recovering from a hard birth. The result of that birthing was currently sitting up in a basket in the corner. The babe's slightly flushed cheeks told her that it was not doing as well as it should, and the farmwife would be doubly glad to see her.

"Welcome mother," the farmwife said warmly, looking up from her bread making. "Come in and seat yourself by the fire. I'll bring you a little something to eat and drink in just a moment."

She set her basket down near the door. "Don't be silly! I'll help you. Then the task will be done all the sooner and we both can take a rest."

While they worked, the farmwife proceeded to tell her of all the troubles the new babe had been having (which the eld woman had guessed already) and the strangeness of the weather (which she had seen for herself).

"It's not just the weather, or my little Jan being sick. There's been an ill air about us since just after last harvest," the farmwife concluded, setting the loaves to the side. "I was thinking of putting an extra bowl out on the stoop at night, for the Good Folk. It will do no harm, and perhaps even change our fortune for the better."

"Maybe. But I will leave you with some of the medicinals that I have brought all the same." Dusting off her hands, she reached into the basket that she had brought, pulling from it a bag full of herbs and a small jar of salve. She gave these to the farmwife, all the while instructing her on how to make infusions for the baby and urging her to rub the salve on all the family's chests, should the need arise. She also gifted the young wife with a spray of herbs tied up neatly in a red string; a charm meant to help protect those in the house from ill airs and harmful spirits.

"Thank you thrice over, mother! Your visits and help are always welcome. Please take this," the farmwife said, handing her a jar of barley syrup. "We can also spare a bag of oats and two of barley, can't we love?" She asked her husband who was just coming in through the door.

"We have plenty, and you are welcome to it," said the farmer. "Though I can't say if it will be true in the year to come."

"If you would hear some advice, then I would say it may be that oats are a better choice this year than barley," she suggested. "They don't mind a wetter field."

"Your wisdom is always appreciated, good henwife," said the farmer, nodding his head.

She followed him out as he loaded the sacks of grain into her barrow. While they spoke, she cast her eye about for Thom and was surprised to see him still at the butter churn, now churning away happily. The hound at his side looked at her in such a way that she feared the stories the children might tell their elders once she and her companions were gone.

"That is a fine boy you have there!" the farmwife said from where she stood in the doorway. "Is he kin to you?"

"He's a fosterling," she answered. It was the truth after all.

"He is a handsome one, and what a head of hair. As golden as a field in the autumn, and those eyes! I have never seen such a bright clear color," the farmwife exclaimed. "He has an air about him, like a king's, it is. Had I one like him, I would be afraid of him being stolen away by the faeries."

"He's more like to be a woodcutter than a king," the eld woman scoffed. She said nothing of faeries, even while the phooka sitting next to the boy laughed knowingly at her with his hound's grin.

They left soon after that. The eld woman taking up the handles of the barrow once again. Turning out onto the muddy lane, she continued on towards the next homestead.

As soon as they were well away, far enough so that she was sure that there were no unwanted ears around to overhear them, she turned and spoke to the phooka beside her.

"The twinkle in your eye tells me you have something to say."

"Ah, you know me so well," he teased, his words bubbling up with mirth.

"Well, you might as well say it then, before you do yourself a mischief," she said. "And preferably before we get to the next homestead." Though truth be told, the next homestead was still a far distance off.

"Oh, I'm pretty sure I'll do myself a mischief by saying it!" he chortled, which was quite the sight coming from his hound's face.

"No doubt, I am sure," she concurred.

"Since you say I am doomed either way… tell me this, don't you share the good farmwife's concern?"

"Which concern should I share?" she asked.

"Why being stolen away by fairies, of course."

"Stolen away by fairies?" she snorted. She should have known it would be something outrageous. "It's a little late for me to be worried about you stealing me away."

"Ah, but I would gladly steal you away, if you wanted me to," he promised her quite earnestly.

"No, you would not," she said, scowling in his direction.

"You could be a fairy bride," he reasoned, undaunted by the look she gave him.

"No, I could not!" she insisted, her tone growing sharper as her cheeks grew warmer. Damn him for making her blush like a maid. "Watch yourself phooka, before I tie your tongue in a knot!"

He laughed outright then, and in the next moment he stood before her as a man. The barrow coming to a stop as he leaned towards her over the front of it.

"Promises, promises. And just how would you tie my tongue in a knot?" he asked with a smile and a quick dodge as she swatted at him. Changing to a hound again as he bounded away, laughing all the while as he wisely stayed well out of her reach.

There was no one in the fields or the yard when they arrived at the next farm, but she could hear the cow lowing in the barn. The bleating sheep still enclosed in their pen moved restlessly about. She left the barrow in the middle of the yard.

"Stay here," she told the two who were with her. Taking up her basket, she made her way to the door and knocked briskly. A coughing was coming from inside, loud enough for her to hear it even through the closed door. The farmer himself opened it, looking bleary-eyed, haggard and unshaven.

"Spaewife!" he exclaimed, his tired eyes lighting up at the sight of her. "Never have I been happier to see someone. My Mary and the little ones have been sick for days and just this morning my oldest boy took to his bed."

She followed the farmer into the house. The air was stale and smelled of sickness. The large room's only bed was taken up by the farmer's wife, who had their youngest tucked up next to her, while two other little ones lay on a pallet on the floor beside her. The farmer's eldest had a pallet of his own which had been drawn up close to the fire. Their labored breathing was harsh in her ears. One and all had the flushed cheeks she would expect from a fever.

She set about her work, unpacking what she needed from her basket and heating water for the plasters and tisanes. The farmer stayed at her side while she worked, worry and fatigue chasing over his features like storm clouds.

"Get some rest if you can," she told him.

"No time," he said. "It's near midday and the milking isn't done and the sheep are still penned. Thank heaven we finished the shearing, early as it was..." The farmer let out an angry moan. "No, you are not welcome, Grimm. You can't have them!"

Turning quickly, she found a familiar black hound sitting in the doorway.

"Peace! He is mine and means no harm," she reassured the farmer. "I had left him and my fosterling in the yard, when I came to see what was troubling your house." At that, the hound stood up, tail wagging as he headed back out into the yard. Belatedly she realized what it was she had said. Berating herself soundly, she returned to her work. She was sure claiming him as she had would bring her no end of trouble.

"He is a fearsome beast," the farmer said warily, heading out himself only to stop in the doorway. "Blue skies above, I don't believe it!" His exclamation drew her from her task, wiping her hands, she came to stand at the door beside him.

There on the stoop were two full pails of milk. The sheep and the cow could be seen further out in the pasture, Thom standing not far away with the hound at his side. The impertinent hound who turned and winked at her.

She put her hand on the farmer's arm, urging him back in the house and towards a pallet in the corner. "Come rest. My fosterling will keep watch and I dare say you will find your barn clean once you have woken." He did as she bid, too dumbstruck to argue.

The day wore on into night. She checked on Hoax and the boy often, making sure they had food and were comfortably bedded down in the barn. Although it was long after midnight before she came to join them.

The barn was as spotless as she had predicted it would be, the phooka's nature being what it was. Bone-weary, she climbed up into the loft to find Thom wrapped in a blanket, fast asleep in the sweet-smelling hay. The hound lay next to him, his head resting across the boy's legs. A feeling of warm contentment settled over her at the sight of them there. So much so, that her heart felt almost over-full with the emotion.

Neither stirred when she wrapped herself up in the blanket that had been thoughtfully left for her. Their gentle snores were her lullaby as she surrendered herself to the welcome oblivion that awaited her.

By late the following morning, the littlest ones were much improved, and the farmer's wife and oldest son were already back on their feet.

"My thanks, spaewife," the farmer said as he loaded two bags of oats and three of wool into her barrow. "It is little enough that I can offer for all that you have done, but please take it and welcome," he said, adding to it a large wheel of cheese.

She made sure to leave them with plenty of herbs and instructions on how to use them, as well as a large bottle of syrup made from elderberries and honey, which she had brought with her. Wishing them well she set off, pushing the now much heavier barrow back down the lane they had come up the day before.

It wasn't easy. The mud was thick, sticky stuff and often caused the barrow to slip down into the ruts where it was thicker still. She was grateful when Thom came up along-side to help. The cart began to move with uncanny ease. Looking over her shoulder, she found a grinning phooka behind her, holding onto the ends of the barrow's long handles.

Had he been expecting her to argue, he was to be sore-ly disappointed. She was not too proud to accept help, and was certainly too tired at the moment to complain when help was given unasked for. He stopped the barrow, allowing her to slip out from between the handles, before taking them back up again. He began to push it along with a jaunty step.

"'He is mine and means no harm' she says, claiming me in front of all and sundry," the phooka preened, proving that she had been right when she thought that her casual words would bring her all sorts of trouble.

"A single farmer is hardly 'all and sundry'," she informed him.

"That might be true," the phooka agreed without agreeing at all. "And what good's a claiming without a name. He certainly did not have yours, or one could say he had many of yours: spaewife, henwife, eld woman, herb woman. How many names do you have?"

"More than I can remember," she admitted. "Names have power as you well know, even names such as those."

"So they do, so they do. But not so much as the one I would call you. I wonder, would you give me that one if I asked you nicely?" His words were light and full of mischief, but she could not say the same for his eyes.

"You know it, and have for as long as your king has," she replied in kind, her words without weight. Though she felt unsteady having found herself all at sea again with this creature she had known for so long.

"I do know it, but you have never given it to me. Knowing a name is not the same as having been given a name," he pointed out.

She could not argue against that.

"Our Lady of the Glade gave hers freely enough when first we met her," he cajoled.

"Because she is a guileless creature who knew no better. She would never think to use such a thing against someone and therefore never thought to have a care with hers," she concluded.

"And am I not guileless?" he asked, turning wide eyes her way. The tips of his pony ears drooped in a most harmless fashion as his full lips did their best to convince her of his innocent intentions. All of which she knew to be a lie.

"You are guile itself, you mischievous devil," she said, smiling at him despite herself.

"Ah, you know me so well," he said, his pitiful expression vanishing like fairy gold in the morning light.

"I do, though I still don't know why lately you've become determined to devil me so," she groused.

"Lost," observed Thom from where he was walking

with one hand on the edge of the barrow. His brilliant cyanic eyes looked directly at Hoax.

"There is no doubt you have the sight my friend, though sometimes you see too much," the phooka said cheerfully.

The bright sun continued to beat down on them as they made their way back home. Exhaustion dragged at her heels as she walked next to the barrow, a result of yesterday's labors, she was sure.

When they arrived at the house at wood's edge, Hoax pushed the barrow around to the side where the spring was without her even asking. On that same side was a lean-to where she kept a mill for grinding grain. Its wooden handle, worn from long use, stuck straight up from the topmost of the two stones, waiting for her hand to start it turning.

Grinding grain into flour was a chore she usually enjoyed, but at that moment just the thought of it was daunting. So, she left one sack of oats and one of barley beside the mill for later. The bags of wool went next to them. That would have to be washed and dried before it would be ready for carding. Another task that she was a little too tired to think about just then.

She turned to see Hoax grab two of the remaining bags of grain left in the barrow while directing Thom to grab the last. Her aching back blessed them for their thoughtfulness. Grabbing the wheel of cheese and jar of barley syrup, she had them follow her through the outside door that led to the spring cellar and the pantry just beyond. She sent them on ahead to where the pantry was, while she headed down the handful of steps into the spring cellar.

The coolness of the room was welcome after the unrelenting sun of the journey home. She put the jar of barley syrup up on one shelf and the cheese on another, taking stock as she did so. What she had there would have lasted her for quite some while, with the possible exception of the cream; the silver cat having a particular love of it. But now she doubted her supplies would last much more than a month.

It had taken very little to keep herself clothed, fed and comfortable. The wood usually provided her with most of what she needed and her visits to the crofts provided the rest. And should she need something neither could give, there was always the goblin market where she could find anything her heart desired, as long as she had something equally precious to offer in exchange.

But things were much different now, and in the dimness of the spring cellar she could allow herself to admit that they were difficult. She wondered what these past few weeks would have been like had Hoax not been there. Would she have been up to the task of taking care of Thom on her own? She did not know, but it certainly would have been harder without him. She shook her head; what use were such speculations anyway? Taking a deep breath, she settled her shoulders, dismissing those things she could do nothing about at the moment. Bending down, she looked into the crocks where she kept the cream, milk and butter.

"You were gone forever," said the silver cat, having appeared from nowhere beside her.

"We were gone for a day," she corrected him.

"The crock with the cream is in the water," the silver cat pointed out, his tail tapping across his front paws in annoyance. Which was true, the stoneware holding the cream was right in the middle of the channel of cold water that ran along one side of the floor.

"So it is!" she said, smiling at the indignant look the silver cat gave her.

"I can't reach it, if it is in the water."

"Which is probably the only reason I have any left," she remarked, reaching over to stroke his soft fur. "Besides, the kitchen in the goblin's Keep is filled with food, and the shopkeepers in the market give you fish whenever you pass by, in the hopes of currying favor from your mistress, no doubt."

"Yes. But that is there, and I am here. And you were gone forever."

She picked him up, which was not something he always let her do.

"I forgive you," he assured her, sliding his whiskered cheek along her jaw. A soft purr rumbling in his throat.

"You forgive me," she chuckled fondly. "Now you just sound like that ridiculous phooka."

The silver cat gave a soft sneeze and jumped down from her arms. "Well, if you're going to be insulting..." he said, walking away with his tail held high.

She followed him back outside where she found Hoax sitting beneath the wild cherry tree with his eyes closed.

Thom lay curled up on the ground, close beside him. The late afternoon sun fell through the snowy white blooms, gathering into little aureate pools all around them. The same warm feeling she had felt the night before washed over her again, and even the doubts that haunted her could not lessen it.

She left them where they were, making her way back into the cottage. Inside, next to the table, she found all the grain she had set aside already ground into the finest flour. Her fatigue vanished. She did not know how the phooka had managed such a feat in the minuscule amount of time she had been in the spring cellar, but she was grateful for the help. With a much lighter heart, she set about making honey cakes.

Thom and the phooka wandered in just as she was finishing up making dinner. Thom went to sit at the table while Hoax stretched out near the hearth, not quite underfoot, but close to it.

She could tell he was quite pleased with himself. Of course, she did not thank him for the work he had done; he was what he was, after all. Instead, she placed two honey cakes on a plate, and poured the last of the milk into an earthenware bowl. She set both on the hearthstone in front of him, before putting the remainder of the dinner on the table for herself and Thom.

Hoax sat up to eat and drink the offering that was left for him, a twinkle in his eye as he watched her.

When the eld woman went out the next morning to fill the kettle from the spring, she found three plump black hens, clucking and scratching happily, in a large yard made of woven willow wands. In addition, the three bags of wool had been washed and carded and now lay out waiting for her in neat roves. She had no doubt that this was the phooka's doing. Whether he did the work himself, she could not say, but it was certainly his doing.

The black hound was still sleeping when she went back into the cottage, on her bedding, of course. She had yet to sleep on the bed that had been gifted to her, choosing instead to continue sleeping in front of the hearth as she had been. The phooka never mentioned it, seemingly content to curl up on the feather ticking next to her every night.

This morning she could not bring herself to shoo him off as she usually would. Instead she carefully made her way around him, stirring up the fire to heat the kettle and warm up the honey cakes from the night before.

It was some while later that the silver cat wandered out from the bedroom, joining the phooka where he slept.

"I noticed you have no qualms about sleeping on the new bed," she noted to the silver cat who merely flicked an ear in her direction by way of an answer. After laying the food out on the table, she went in to wake Thom.

She found him as she did many mornings now, staring out of the window. Taking up her silver brush from the washstand, she stood behind him and began to undo the night tangles from his thick hair. It was a quiet moment, the rhythmic movement of the brush;

the silken fall of the golden strands bringing with it a measure of peace. She looked over the top of his head out the same window he did, wondering again what it was he watched for. The deep woods drew her eye out through the garden and beyond the gorse hedge, yellow with flowers, to the brilliant shadows beyond. The boy began singing softly to himself, a lilting melody she was sure no mortal had ever written. A soft sigh escaped as she considered the boy in front of her, unsure of how to help him or whether he even wanted her to.

A few endless moments later the silver cat came wandering back in, making pointed remarks about breakfast or the lack thereof.

The eld woman wrapped her arms around Thom's shoulders, giving him a brief hug before leaving to feed the incorrigible cat and see if an equally incorrigible phooka was awake.

The morning was still young when they started out through the goblins' wood, Hoax obligingly carrying her and Thom on his strong pony back. Not that he did so quietly, seeming to take great delight in bantering back and forth with the silver cat, and occasionally needling her in turn. The sounds of merriment and sharp rebuke resonated through the hushed world beneath the familiar branches of oak and wych-elm, until they came to the edge of the wood. Beyond the trees' dark trunks, she could see a wall of shimmering gold cutting like a blade of light through the twilit land in which they walked. It marked the break in the trees where the border stream stood as a boundary between the wood they were in and the fairies' wood just beyond.

The phooka carried them out from the soft shadows into the fall of light. The stream in front of them was still broader than it should have been, stretching well beyond its banks. Hoax stopped at the edge. She felt a slight ripple in his muscles, then they were floating over the shining ribbon of water as gently as thistledown.

On the other side, Hoax carried them to where she saw the red-speckled hides of fairy cattle moving through the tree shade. He stopped not far from the place where the glastig who was minding the herd stood, her dainty hooves peeking out from beneath the hem of a dress which was the same color as the fiddleheads at her feet.

The eld woman slid down, leaving the boy with Hoax and the silver cat. She made her way over to a fallen log that looked a likely seat, waving to the goblin woman as she went. Once she had made herself comfortable, the glastig's sweet-tempered charges came to her one by one to be milked. The pail which she used, a gift from Lorne, was soon half full, but never grew any fuller no matter how much milk she added, and she added quite a bit. She would have plenty now, enough even for cheese and butter. The cream from the fairy cattle tasted as sweet as honey, and she hoped that Thom would find it appealing.

As she was waiting for the next cow to come to her, she looked over to where Hoax, now a great black hound, was minding Thom. He was doing so mostly by fetching sticks the boy had not thrown, in the hopes that he might. The phooka even went as far as to throw the stick himself before changing into a hound to fetch it. It was both amusing, and infinitely sad to watch.

"It seems as though there may be something missing in their game," said the silver cat who was sitting next to her as she went about her chore, to make it easier for her to share the milk with him, no doubt. "In fact, it seems the whole of this wood is dull for the lack of something."

She looked around them then. The wood in which they now sat was a part of the fairy wood and as such beholden to the Fairy Queen, cursed though she may be. The sun in the new beech leaves above set them aglow with emerald fire. The ephemeral flowers of spring carpeted the land around them, infusing the wind with their sweet scent as it blew through the trees. It was lovely, but she could see what it was that the silver cat referred to. For all its loveliness, it was the same as any mortal wood. It was missing that which made it more and its mortality was showing itself. The same mortality she now felt in her own bones. A nose nudged gently at her shoulder bringing her mind back to the task at hand.

"Yes, yes, I know," she said to the cow, placing the pail where it needed to be. Resting her head against the soft, red-speckled flank, she turned her mind back to her chore, and let the rest of her concerns go for the time being.

Once all the milking was done, the herd moved on. But she continued sitting where she was a while longer, watching the boy who was currently crouched down amongst the cowslips and wood anemone. The silver cat had wandered over at some point to sit beside him, so that now they were both peering intently at something beneath the leaves. Hoax, having worn himself out, lay panting in a nearby sunbeam.

A flash of white in the deeper shadows of the trees caught her eye, the fleeting glimpse of a moon-white flank. Smiling, she waited for the White Stag to appear, thinking of a few choice things she wished to tell him. Mostly about his wayward knight who had come to live with her and was even now lazing in the sun. She continued waiting until said wayward knight came to join her, abandoning his hound shape for his more human one as he settled next to her in the shade.

"Did you expect to see your king in these woods today?" she asked him.

"Not at all," the phooka replied. "Even though the throne in Underhill sits empty, he still prefers not to roam here, given the choice."

"Hmm, I wonder if there's someone looking to cause mischief then?" she speculated aloud to herself.

"Mischief in the woods? If that's what you are looking for then I think myself a fine choice," he whispered leaning closer to her as though sharing a secret.

"If it's mischief I am looking for, then you would be the only one to pick, no doubts," she replied absently.

"I am delighted to hear it!"

The echo of a chime rang through the air, interrupting anything else the phooka might have been about to say. His head came up, the tips of his pony ears pricking forward. She had only turned her eyes away from the boy for a moment yet looking around she could find no trace of him.

"It seems our little bird has flown off again," Hoax said as he stood, taking up the pail in one hand and reaching out to take her hand with his other. She stood with him and together they set out, following the sound that would lead them to their wayward boy.

They found Thom in front of a tall boulder that stood in the center of an old hazel grove; his hand resting next to a great split that ran straight through the boulder's heart, from top to bottom.

"The door is closed," he proclaimed sadly.

"So it is," Hoax agreed, not sounding sad at all.

She watched the boy turn away silently and leave the grove by a different path than the one by which they had entered. She and Hoax followed closely behind him. The grove seemed vaguely familiar to her, now that she had a moment to take notice, as did the sea of bluebells the boy led them through. But it wasn't until she saw the glade in front of her, with the drowned meadow and lake just beyond, that she understood why.

Spring had done much to repair the damage wrought by the fire last autumn, but some signs remained still. The charred trunk of a rowan tree atop scorched rocks was a stark reminder of that tragedy; however, hope could be found in the young sapling growing at its foot.

Its thin arms were covered with new green leaves whose color matched the hair of the Rowan Maiden who was resting happily beneath them. The silver cat lounged not far away from her with his mistress beside him. The Lady of the Glade, standing no higher than a dandelion stalk, waved at them in greeting.

Hoax let go her hand and went to kneel before his queen, managing somehow to be irreverent in his reverence.

"I am surprised to see you here, fair one. Have you tired of my King already?"

Lumina laughed fondly at him. "And I am surprised that the eld woman has not sent you home already," she said, smiling at them both.

"Oh, I am sure she would like to. But I am hoping that she will find a use for me yet," he quipped, winking wickedly back over his shoulder at her.

Despite the phooka's tendency towards needling her, the eld woman had to admit the rest of the day was a peaceful one. She took great pleasure in seeing the obvious joy Lumina felt in sharing with them how much her glade had recovered. And it seemed the land around them preened under its mistress's praise, so much so that the air itself gleamed. It was a vivid contrast to the dullness of the wood they had just come from.

It was well past midday when they left Lumina's merry company. They returned home in the warm haze of a golden afternoon, and the eld woman soon set to work skimming the cream from the top of the milk. Most of it went to Thom who happily began to churn it into butter. Some of what was left, she set near the hearth with the plans that she would make cheese with it. The rest was poured into earthenware crocks to be used later. She put the phooka to work carrying them to the spring cellar. He did so cheerfully, though she suspected a few were lighter by the time they had made it there, payment taken for a job well done.

It was later than was usual by the time they got around to eating, but she thought the dinner was well worth the wait. There was fresh butter to go with hot kettle bread and cheese sliced from the wheel given to her by the farmer. Dried pears, soaked in cider and covered in cream, rounded off the feast.

Thom went to bed soon after the meal was finished. She followed suit, finding herself exhausted by the time she finally laid down in front of the hearth. The house was quiet save for the steady breathing of the hound curled up behind her. The fire crackled faintly as the salamanders slipped through the glowing coals.

Still, sleep was a long time coming. She knew, though she had not been told, that the door in front of which Thom had stood led to Underhill, and that image had settled like a cold weight in the pit of her stomach. It filled her with a vague dread that followed her down into fitful dreams.

CHAPTER 4

Lost Ones

Summer flowers wreathed around Winter's head while the angry moon looked down from above. Contagious fogs crept across the land, their cold tendrils slipping through windows and under doors. Thom stood, dry-eyed, before the door to Underhill while the trees around him cried, their leaves falling like tears. The mournful ringing of the hedge bells grew louder and louder…

It was the sound of ringing that pulled her from her dreams. She woke to a cold house and a wide-open front door. The bedding beside her was empty of the hound who had been curled up there when she had fallen asleep. And for some reason she could not fathom, that fact made her angry.

As it turned out, the insistent sound she heard was not coming from the hedge bells at all, but rather from the clapperless ones encircling her wrist. She got to her feet stiffly and made her way to the open door. In its shadow she found the hound, his glowing eyes hooded as he stared out into the icy fog that crept over the ground. She could see Thom beyond him, standing at the garden gate. The breath in her throat froze when she saw the creature waiting just on the other side of him.

The hind's coat, as white as a budding hawthorn, shone bright beneath the veiled moon. She stood there, a dream made flesh, her unearthly beauty shattered by the very human despair in her wide eyes. The mist, in its kindness, rose up to envelope the exiled queen, hiding her from mortal sight and the eld woman's pitying gaze.

She left the doorway and made her way out towards where Thom still stood at the gate, unwrapping the shawl from around herself as she went. There was a quiet rustle of feathers before a familiar weight settled on her shoulder.

"So the Fairy Queen haunts him still," Hoax observed, preening back a strand of her hair. "I'm sorry to leave you, my prickly witch, but I feel that this is something He must know about." And she knew that the 'He' the phooka spoke of was the Goblin King.

"Of course," she said, wrapping her shawl around Thom's shoulders. The raven hopped from her shoulder to the gate, then set off, winging his way through the trees and out over the moors. Turning Thom gently around, she guided him back towards the house.

When the morning sun finally rose, it was greeted by a world garbed in icy splendor. The red roses growing at her window were edged in frost, as was the rest of the garden, each leaf and petal laced in sparkling white. The fog from the night before still gathered in the hollows of the ground, little clouds come down to earth. It was beautiful but boded ill for the year to come.

Thom sat amidst the frigid beauty, barefooted and without a coat, singing to the wind and laughing at jokes only he could hear. There was nothing that she could do about it short of dragging him inside by his collar. Which truth be told, she was tempted to do, her temper that morning being shorter than was usual. Unfortunately, the day did not improve as it aged. The general malaise that had settled over her only grew worse, until noon found her huddled in her wing chair where she usually sat to sew. Thom was sitting on a cushion on the floor beside her, his head leaning against her knee. Her eyelids continued to slide closed no matter how she tried to keep them open, as though the weight of the world rested on their lashes. Knowing that the boy was right there, safe, she surrendered to sleep.

A gentle touch intruded on the nothingness, calling her up from the depths of sleep. She noticed an absence of the warmth that had been Thom's cheek on her knee, and panic took hold, startling her fully awake. She found a pair of amber gold eyes looking down softly at her.

"There's no need for worry," Lumina reassured her. "Thom is safe. The silver cat is keeping him company while he plays with the sylphs."

She released the breath that she had not realized she had been holding. Lumina patted her arm and went over to sit at the table. The eld woman levered herself up from the chair and went to put the kettle on for tea, more out of habit than any real desire for it. She set the teapot out on the table and took down her china cup and the blue thimble as she always did, only to have to turn back and replace the thimble, grabbing a second cup from the hook.

She was used to fae and goblin alike changing their shape and size on a whim. But at that moment her head felt as if it was filled with cotton, and she was so used to her friend being no more than a hands-breadth high that she had done as she normally would without thinking.

"You are not yourself," Lumina observed, taking the proffered cup and setting it down in front of her. "Sit and let me make the tea for once."

The sprite was up and looking through the containers of teas and tisanes on the shelf above before the eld woman could even think to argue. She watched Lumina pull out a small porcelain box from behind the others; the sight of it brought a small smile to her lips. How interesting that the sprite should pick that one, given that it had been a gift from Lorne the previous summer.

The tea was added to the pot with hot water from the kettle following closely after. Ginger-scented steam curled up from the spout. They let it steep while they watched Thom through the window. He was sitting in the sun, but unlike earlier, he had on a coat and shoes to keep the cold air off of him.

The frost from that morning had long since melted, leaving much of the garden around him wilted and bruised. He was playing with the sylphs, just as Lumina had said, holding up blackened leaves for them to take from his fingers. They set them to swirling around him, a whirlwind of dying foliage with him and the silver cat at its center. Occasionally, the silver cat would reach up and snatch one from the air. A sadness washed over her at the sight of Thom smiling at the sylphs as they laughed and danced around him. Perhaps it was knowing that to anyone else it would appear as if he was looking at nothing at all.

"You worry about him."

She turned her gaze from outside to look at her companion who was pouring the tea and watching her with troubled eyes.

"I do," she admitted with a sigh. She seemed to be sighing a lot lately, either in resignation or exasperation. Often times both, if the phooka was involved.

"Why," Lumina asked.

Hoax had asked a similar question not so long ago. She was finding it no easier now than she had then to explain her fears of the future to someone for which time held little meaning.

"Because the hidden world is so much more real to him that I worry he cannot see the dangers of the mortal one in which he lives," she explained. "And what of when he is grown? It will happen much faster than you realize, and there may come a day when he chooses to walk solely in the world of men. He may have to forsake you, and all of us, to do so. And even then, he will not be as others are no matter what his choice and I fear he will face their persecution because of it."

"Why would he not just stay here?" Lumina asked. "Live between the worlds as you do?"

"It may be that he will. But living between worlds means shunning the company of mortals, for the most part, and there may come a time when he no longer wishes to."

She watched the boy as he sang; fear, worry and doubt warring against each other in her heart. The worry of not being able to protect him and the need to know he was safe if he were to leave at odds with the understanding of what it meant to care for someone who could not care for themselves. The endless years of Thom's life spooled out before her, and with it came the crushing weight of what such a commitment entailed.

A soft hand covered hers. "I am sorry, my friend." Lumina's face was concerned and thoughtful as it looked into hers. "I think that I did not understand the burden that I asked you to shoulder. It seems that is twice now that I have done you harm without intending to."

For the briefest moment, her treacherous heart wanted to agree. But, she knew that to be wrong. It had been her choice to give Lumina the last apple from the old apple tree, knowing full well what it would cost her. And she had agreed to take in Thom, knowing that he would have a hard path before him. Both choices had been hers to make and she had made them from the heart, so she knew them to be right. However, knowing that did not always make the consequences of those choices any easier to bear.

"Have I done him more harm than good?" the gentle sprite asked, her worry made plain to the eld woman by the unshed tears she could see in Lumina's eyes.

"No," she replied despite her own doubts. "And what choice was there, really? At least you, over all others, had only his best interests in mind. For the Fairy Queen, the boy was just a pawn, to be used against the Goblin King."

"Do you really feel that to be so? I have often wondered if retribution was truly all that motivated the Fairy Queen," Lumina speculated. "I was told the white hind came to your gate and Thom was there waiting. I do not believe that she ever meant to do the boy harm, and there is no doubt in my mind that she once loved Lorne and his brother."

"Your assessment of her is far kinder than mine," the eld woman noted, her woolly head smothering any sympathy she may have felt.

"So the silver cat frequently tells me," Lumina said ruefully. "But the heart is never a simple thing."

What could she say to that? Her own world had been stood on its head. And if she were honest with herself, it might be more the fault of the phooka that was conveniently absent, than the boy who was out in her garden talking to the wind.

"That is undoubtedly true," she agreed. "Still, I feel the doom Lorne placed on Maeve was just, and far more lenient than any I would have pronounced. Even as soft-hearted as you are my friend, I can't believe that you don't feel the same."

"You are right. I have no forgiveness for the Fairy Queen," Lumina admitted. "But I have no ill will either. My husband and I were of the same mind when he bound her to her fate. Had we not been, he could not have called down such a judgment. It was because the wrongs had been done to both of us that it had such power, though the wrong done to him was worse by far than any I suffered." Her face turned thoughtful. "But I am of a mind that such judgments are not always about punishment. They can open paths that you may have never known were there otherwise. They can be a chance to change your fate. I wonder if in time the Fairy Queen will see that."

"I very much doubt it," the eld woman said.

Hoax had still not returned by the time Lumina left, so it had been only her and Thom for dinner. The meal was a simple one of cheese and bread from the day before since she could not bring herself to be bothered making anything else.

She had pulled her wing chair closer to the hearth, thinking the heat would chase off the constant chill she felt, but it was not working as she had hoped. Thom was sitting at her feet again, softly humming to the salamanders that were dancing in the flames. Steam rose up from another cup of ginger lemon tea that she was holding in her lap. She breathed it in slowly as it wreathed her face.

The feeling that had plagued her all day became even stronger as evening fell. Her muscles ached and her head felt like it was floating above her shoulders rather than sitting on them. There was no doubt in her mind that she was sick. She should have realized it sooner. But it had been so long since she had last been ill she had not recognized the signs.

She must have nodded off, because when next she opened her eyes, she found Thom standing in front of her. Reaching out, he placed his hand on her forehead. "Hot," he said, then left.

To her surprise, he came back fairly quickly, carrying the blanket from off the bed. She lifted her cup out of the way as he draped it across her lap, tucking it in between her and the chair. She smiled up at him.

"Thank you," she said as a profound fatigue settled over her. "Please don't go wandering Thom." Patting her hand, he sat down again at her feet, his head resting on her knee.

Sleep refused to be denied as it wrapped her in its embrace, and she doubted she could have stopped it even if the world itself was breaking. The fever dreams grabbed hold of her and held on tight, pulling her in deeper and deeper in every time she tried to claw her way out of them. The sun and the moon were dancers, spinning through a darkened wood while golden-haired princes chased after white hinds, and silver cats patted her cheek, telling her that she needed to wake up.

She woke to cool darkness and soft sheets under her cheek. It was deepest night. The room's windows were outlined in silver by the moon's thin light. She was tucked into the bed that had been gifted to her, but in which she had never slept. A phooka-shaped shadow was bathing her forehead with a damp cloth that smelled of chamomile and lavender.

"Hoax," she croaked through dry lips that would not come apart as they should.

"Finally awake, are you?" he breathed. "Don't try to speak."

A finger softly smoothed over her lips leaving honey in its wake. It was followed by something cool and wet pressing against her mouth.

"It is only a small piece of fruit," he assured her.

Opening her lips she accepted what he offered. If it was fruit, it was like none she had ever tasted before, juicy and sweet as candy. It soothed the water-starved tissues of her mouth.

She continued to eat the small bits of fruit he gave her without complaint, too tired to muster up the outrage she should have felt. He fed her quietly, carefully until the fruit was gone. They had known each other for what would have been many of her lifetimes, yet the creature sitting on the floor next to her bed was entirely new to her. A stranger with whom she was deeply familiar, and her addled brain was finding it hard to reconcile the devil-may-care rogue who always took great delight in her vexation with the serious creature caring for her so gently.

"You are not the one I would have expected at my bedside," she said, her voice much less rough now.

"Who else other than me; the silver cat?" he asked quietly. "Unless you think a larder stocked with frogs and mice would make you feel better? Even my master has been too long from his roots to remember the fragility of a mortal shell. I, on the other hand, have plowed their fields and tended their animals when they could not. And have long watched you nurse them, though you never knew it."

He lifted first one hand, then the other, drawing the damp cloth along her fingers. Turning it over, so the cool wetness brushed along her wrist and over her palm. It came to her then, in the clarity that sickness often brings, just who had been responsible for making sure Thom had what he needed at midwinter.

"You chose the gifts at Yule," she surmised.

"I pointed out what might be needed," he conceded. "The only gift I gave was the one I wrapped around your shoulders."

The soft warm shawl she had been given this winter… the bed she now slept in… "What will be the price for all these gifts?" she wondered aloud.

"Do all gifts need to come with a price?" he asked, smoothing his hand over her hair, brushing back the strands that whispered across her forehead.

"With mortals, most often. With the Good Folk, always," she replied.

"So jaded," he said, the white of his smile shining in the dark. "But not necessarily wrong."

"Why have you really come to live here?" she asked, suddenly wanting very much to know.

"Why, to win your heart, dear witch. What other reason would I need?" He answered her with all seriousness. His words, quiet and intent, fell like petals on water into the night's stillness.

"Infuriating creature," she sighed. It seemed that he was not as different as she had thought him to be, and maybe it was only her illness and the strangeness of the night that gave depth to words that had none. "I know better than to expect a straight answer from you, but I do expect a true one."

"And once again you make assumptions so that you might hide behind them," he said with uncommon sternness as he returned to bathing her face. The damp cloth stroking gently over her too-tight skin.

"Do I? No doubt you will tell me what they are," she rasped, leaning into the coolness as it glided over her cheek. He held a cup up to her lips.

"No doubt," he agreed, the white crescent of his smile flashing again in the dark. "You pretend that there is only one answer to a question when in fact, such is almost never true. Still I know the answer you wish to hear, and it is true in part, so I will give it to you... My king has found his heart again in the form of a sweet-eyed sprite and so my duties to him are much reduced."

"And so you feel that he has no need for you," she reasoned.

"Just so," he agreed, and his voice once again held the merry teasing that she was so accustomed to. "I am now a rudderless ship without a destination. 'Lost' as our boy so aptly put it. So I thought why should I not come here to live with the other lost ones?"

"Lost ones are we?" she harrumphed, regretting it instantly as her chest buzzed with a cough that never came.

"Oh yes dearheart, most certainly!" The cloth had disappeared to be replaced by gentle fingers applying a familiar smelling salve on her chest in slow circles. "For the boy has lost his dreams and you have gained your mortality, if only for a time, which could be seen as a very great loss indeed. And since, as you have most helpfully pointed out, I am now without my reason, who else's doorstep should I darken but yours?"

"And that is your answer?" she said resignedly,

"It is, though the first answer I gave you was just as true," the phooka affirmed as his thumb smoothed honey gently over her lips again. "Perhaps one day, you will be ready to hear all the truths in my answers."

Hoax sat with her through the night, stealing away just as the first light of day touched the sky. He assured her before he went that everything was in hand and that she should rest, but such dubious reassurance only convinced her that she should get up out of bed. And it was with that thought in mind that she fell even more deeply asleep.

When she was finally able to wake fully, she found the sun streaming through the window, falling across her face and her uncovered toes, which told her that it was already past noon. It was a little disconcerting to realize that she was not sure how many days had passed since she had fallen ill.

She noticed the scent of lavender in the air as she levered herself weakly out of bed. As it turned out, the source of it was coming from behind a screen which had been set up in the corner of the room. There she found steam rising up from a good-sized copper hip bath that had certainly not been there before she had fallen ill. There were even drying cloths folded up on the table next to it, where the pitcher and wash basin still sat.

She would not let herself think too hard on how it had all gotten there. Resigned to the fact that it was here now, she slid off her sweat-stained shift, letting it fall to the floor for washing later. Slowly she lowered herself into the still warm water; it flowed over her, reaching to just about her chest. The tub's back was high enough to allow her to rest her head easily on it and her legs hung comfortably over the bottom edge. A soft cloth, much like the one Hoax had used the night before, hung on the edge of the tub. She used it to wash away the sweat that always came with illness.

A bath such as the one she was in had not existed when she had last lived among mortals, though she had seen its like before in the goblin market. Those had been made of gold though, or silver, or stars from the milky way. The simple farmhouses she visited had a large wooden barrel to bathe in, if they had anything at all. It went to show how much the world had changed since she had last lived among mortal men.

She lingered in the water longer than she had intended, and the water stayed warm all the while. Finally she rose and dried herself off, listening to the voices which carried to her from the other room as she did so. More specifically, the voices of Hoax and the silver cat which sounded quite pleased with themselves. A worrisome thing.

Clean and dry, she dressed and went to see what had become of her household while she had been ill.

When she stepped into the room, it took her eyes a moment to understand what it was they were seeing. Crocks of all shapes and sizes lined the table and nearly every corner had boxes stacked in it. Sacks made of everything from velvet to burlap sat in front of the hearth, if hearth it was. It had been changed beyond recognition, closed in with stone and white clay as it was. Its arched doors, for there were two of them now, yawned open at her like contented cats, while the salamanders happily played in the hearth bottom down below. The green tiles that covered the stove from top to bottom, were only a touch darker than the soft green of the walls, like deeper shade beneath summer leaves.

"What have you two done?" she asked the pair who

were beaming happily at her from amidst the spoils of their endeavors.

"Helping of course," the silver cat informed her. "Though I had wanted to get a cast iron stove; there was one in the market that a prince no longer had any use for, but the phooka pointed out one like this would have warm niches to sleep in."

"I said, niches for keeping things warm in," Hoax corrected him.

"Exactly," agreed the silver cat as though what they had said was one and the same.

"Here," the phooka said, bringing her a chair. "You look as though you need to sit."

They spent the rest of the day proudly showing her everything they had thought she might need, from lost dreams to butterfly wings. Thankfully, somewhere in between those were a few things she could actually use. The silver cat lost interest sometime after he showed her the fish hanging in the spring cellar. The one that was as long as she was tall and which, he happily told her, the shellycoat insisted was from the deepest, coldest sea. That left Hoax to continue on his own until she finally found her voice, which she did as he was showing her twists of shimmering thread nearly invisible to her eye.

"Skeins of spider's thread? What am I to do with those?" she asked, her feelings a pendulum see-sawing between profoundly grateful and slightly horrified. "And here I thought you were one to be practical."

"I am! You need practically everything here." he insisted, eyes twinkling.

In the end, she had to admit much of what Hoax and the silver cat had done was practical. The hearth, as it was now, was very useful. And the undine that lived in the spring had agreed to fill and empty the hip bath, and the water butt as well, in return for the use of the bath on the nights when the full moon was shining. Truth be told, she would find a use for many of the things they had brought.

Later that evening when she had asked the phooka — who was loafing at the foot of the hearth — what the cost for all of it would be, he assured her there would be none. It was merely payment for a debt owed.

CHAPTER 5

The Broken Court

The icy beginning of a few weeks earlier gave way to cooler days that were followed by oddly warm nights. As if the usual late Spring weather had been stood on its head. Plants, ever the optimists, had begun sending out new growth in defiance of the damage done by the frost.

The same could be said for her growing household. With her illness past, a new life had emerged; one filled with helpful cats, incorrigible phookas, and boys in need of tending. She supposed that was how it had already been, but it felt now as though there was an order to the chaos.

She had also found Thom adept at learning to recognize plants and their uses. His sight, much like hers, gave him an understanding of their qualities that others would not have. And the Hidden Folk took great delight in showing him secret places where botanical gems lay hidden on the forest floor. It was of no surprise to her that they would so readily share their knowledge of growing things with him. After all, the Folk love beautiful things, and Thom was a beautiful child who had no fear of them, even when he should.

So, she made a point of teaching him all she could as they wandered through the woods on both sides of the border stream. Anyone else would have been hard pressed to say whether he was listening, but she could tell by the glances he sent her way that he was.

Hoax helped as he had been doing, often tucking Thom into bed in the evenings and keeping an eye on him at other times. He also came with them as they roamed, usually as a hound, but on occasion as the brawny-backed horse who had carried them home that first night. At those times she happily took the opportunity to load him down with their findings. He, in turn, complained loudly, all the while shaking his mane and nudging her shoulder if he thought she was ignoring him. Which of course meant she did ignore him, frequently.

They had headed out that particular morning with the intent of visiting the quiet pond where a urisk lived. For some company and a bit of honeycomb, he was happy to allow her to gather clay from a particularly fine deposit residing in the pond's banks.

The rising sun found them already walking down one of the ancient roads that ran through the goblins' wood. Beside them a bright silver ribbon of a stream tumbled over ebony boulders as it hurried along.

Thom was a little way in front, with Hoax and herself following unhurriedly in his wake. The phooka, as an oddity, was in his human skin, possibly because he was tired of her loading him down with things. Of course, she still had him carrying the large basket which she herself usually carried on her back, so he had not really escaped.

An old bridge loomed just up ahead of where Thom walked. The timeworn arch of its crumbling stones steadfastly spanned the stream's burbling waters. The boy stopped for a moment at the place where the road along which they walked met the one traveling from beyond the bridge. He stood there at the crossways for a little while, facing the weathered moonstone pillar that might have been a cross once, long ago, but was now just a ghost in the gloom of the trees.

She did not know what had caught his attention, but it had not held it for long because he had already continued on by the time she and Hoax had reached the same spot. The sun's thin rays pierced, needle-sharp, through the branches above, falling like little golden coins into the font at the cross's foot. A shimmer of blue held her eye as it raced through the pillar's stone heart, as fleeting as a dream.

"*'First she let the black pass by, and syne she let the brown, But quickly she ran to the milk-white steed and pu'd the rider down'*,[1]" quoted the phooka walking beside her. "And thus, Tamlin's love won his freedom, while his brother suffered his doom. Ah, sweet Janet had you known the pain you and your lover would cause that day, would you have cared? But who am I to complain! For had she not made her bid, the Fairy Queen would still have her Sun and Moon, their hearts captive in her orbit, and myself tethered right along with them."

"That is if she had not already tired of them by now. Either way, it is doubtful you would have known Lumina or her silver cat," she concluded. "And of course, my bones would have been dust in the earth long ago."

"A tragedy above all others!" Hoax declared adamantly.

They had only gone a short way beyond the crossroads when they found a patch of wild strawberries growing in the brightly dappled shade that fell along the bank of the stream. It would usually be too early in the year for them to have berries yet but the whole patch was filled. Their tiny, bright red fruit hung like jewels in the little pools of light. It seemed the strange weather she had been worrying so much about offered at least one benefit.

Hoax took the gathering basket from his back, setting it down at the edge of the road, while she called for Thom to turn around and come join them. She handed each of them a cloth bag from inside the basket, and they set about picking strawberries.

The phooka hopped down to the great black boulders below under the auspice of picking the fruit growing further down on the banks. To her, it looked as though he was only taking the opportunity to amuse himself and get his feet wet. She kept her complaints to herself though since each time he bent down, she saw him add a double handful of berries to the bag he was carrying.

It did not take long for the bags to become full, though she noticed that not all the fruit they gathered made it into them. She straightened up from where she had been bent over, gathering her fair share. Placing her hands on her hips she did her best to stretch the crick out of her back, quite pleased with their progress.

A strong gust of wind set the leaves above to dancing. The light, in turn, darted along the ground in a dizzying whirl, flitting and flashing across the water beside them like a broken mirror in the sun.

Her eyes closed against its brilliance. When she opened them a moment later, Thom was gone.

In the next heartbeat, Hoax was at her side. Grabbing her hand as she set off after the boy. They left bags and basket behind as they, yet again, chased after the wild chiming of clapperless bells.

The sound drew them on, leading them away from the road entirely. Down a seemingly endless green tunnel of brambles they ran; the boy forever ahead of them, as elusive as a deer, or a unicorn of old.

Eventually a hazy circle of light grew up before them marking the place where the labyrinth of greenery finally opened up at a large break in the trees. They stepped out to find Thom standing at the side of a great green mound. It rose up from the clearing floor as smooth as a bowl turned upside down, with not a tree or a bush on it. Its only feature was a door, a plain wooden door with copper hinges set right in the grassy bank in front of him. She thought she saw what might have been a shadow, graceful and lithe, flit over the door's unassuming face just as the boy was reaching out to touch it. It opened easily for him, and he stepped through without hesitation. They followed suit, keeping close on his heels.

In the dim grayness beneath the mound, she could see the thread that connected them all, shining like spun rubies as it stretched out between them. She knew before Hoax stopped that he would, and she could feel his skin twitching like a horse throwing off flies, before he continued on. There was no doubt in her mind that he recognized the wood in which they stood. And she was of half-a-mind that she knew it as well, though she would have never seen it for herself. The trunks of the trees around them were crazed and cracked. Their brittle branches were bare, and all about their feet lay rings of tarnished leaves.

"I once told my king I would happily crush the floors of Underhill beneath my hooves. Grinding them to dust for all that the queen and her court had put him through," Hoax admitted softly from where he stood beside her. His hand, still resting in hers, flexed for a moment then gentled. "But seeing this stretched out before me, I find that I am not happy at all."

"Is that where we are then?" she asked though she had already guessed it to be so.

"Yes. Behold the Shining Court of the Fairy Queen! Where the fairy dance in their rounds and the crystal trees with their silver leaves grow beneath a sky made of lapis. Wonderous Underhill, where all is bright, and shadows never dare to fall."

There was nothing bright about the land they walked through now, though. Eventually the wood fell away, and a great circle opened up ahead of them. Its gloom-haunted edges reached longingly towards its center where a broken throne stood amidst a pile of glittering shards and diamond dust. Thom was standing there in front of it. He turned to look back at them, his eyes bleak but surprisingly lucid.

"The court is broken," he told them, his toneless voice heavy with portent. "The dancers no longer dance, so the world no longer knows which way to turn. Winter thinks it's spring and so does summer. Come autumn there will be no nuts on the trees nor fruits on the bramble. The angry moon hides her face and the vengeful winds bring with them ill airs and contagious fogs from the sea. They swell the rivers and make the lakes forget where their banks should be. Soon the world will forget itself and sickness will stalk us all on silent feet."

His words sent chills through her belly. Still, she found herself smiling, because it was the first time she had heard him string so many of them together.

They had not stayed long in that land of shadows, and yet it was well into the afternoon when they stepped out from Underhill into a familiar grove of hazels.

The gathering basket and bags of strawberries had all been left back near the crossroads, deep in the goblin's wood, which was far and away from where they were now. She was not sure why the doorway had brought them here, instead of where they had entered, but she was sure that there was a reason.

They did not find Lumina in her glade, unlike the last time Thom had led them here. But even in her absence the air shimmered, the colors appearing brighter, as though each petal, leaf and stone had been outlined in light. It was clear that this place was not fully of the mortal world. Which was as it should be and should have been for all of the fairy's wood, but was not.

A gray exhaustion settled over her for no reason that she could discern. "Take us home, Hoax."

"As you wish," he said, changing himself into the dark horse she knew so well.

She helped Thom onto his back and climbed wearily up behind him. Hugging the boy tight, she closed her eyes as the phooka carried them away.

They ate a cold supper that evening, the strangely warm nights making a fire both unnecessary and uncomfortable. Thom and the phooka stayed at the table after the meal was finished to sort through the bags of wild strawberries, which they had miraculously found waiting for them at the gate when they arrived home that afternoon. There were times she could appreciate goblins and their goblin ways.

She left them to it, choosing instead to spin the wool which she had finally had a chance to dye earlier that week. Her mind, relaxed by the soothing click and whir of the spinning wheel, was left to wander and soon turned fanciful as she looked out at the room around her. The glow of the oil lamp lit upon the little piles of berries and transformed them into a horde of rubies scattered across the dark wood of the table. It flickered across the deep green of the walls, conjuring up dancers from the shadows that moved there. The lithe figures whirled through the painted flowers with their gilt-edged leaves, appearing and disappearing in the flame's wavering light.

She saw Underhill's darkened trees in her mind, their tarnished silver leaves lying at their feet. Being mortal, she had never seen the rings of dancers spinning endlessly in the queen's round, though she certainly knew of them. She, herself, used to tell stories to the people of her village long ago. Cautionary tales warning mortals to be wary of joining such rings, lest they find themselves trapped forever in their turning.

But no dancers danced in the queen's round now because there was no queen to call them to do so. The meaning of Thom's words became instantly clear. The world within needed the eternal turning of those wheels. Discord had risen in its absence, and since the faerie and mortal realms moved together, hand-in-hand as lovers do, the lack of one was felt in the other. So now they were showing their displeasure, standing the seasons on their heads, and allowing disease to stalk the world on silent feet. But what to do about it?

Her gaze strayed over to where the boy and phooka sat. A pair of bright green eyes met hers, and she realized that Hoax had been watching her for some time.

"Every kingdom needs a queen," he said as though reading her thoughts.

"That is true," she agreed. However they could not restore the queen that had been, even had they wished it. Lorne had doomed the once Fairy Queen with a mortal heart. A fair punishment, given the harm she had visited on him and Lumina in her desire for a love that she could not understand. But such choices, no matter how just, often brought with them unforeseen repercussions.

"But if the one that was is not to be, then who?" she said aloud, more to herself than anyone else.

Thom lifted his eyes from the strawberries he had been sorting. He did not look at her, nor did he look at the phooka across from him. Instead, his gaze settled on the same wall that she had been looking at. The one where the shifting shadows still whirled like dancers through a painted forest. "The Blue-Rose Woman," was all he said. His attention quickly returned to his task.

Hoax caught her eye again. His were gleaming as he said, "That my boy, is a very interesting idea."

It was not long after that she tucked Thom into bed, snuffing the lamps out as she did so. The darkness rested quietly around her as she sat in her wing chair. A pale moon streamed through the open windows, painting silver squares on the floor. Hoax was sitting just in front of her, ensconced in one of those squares, his fingers idly playing with the moonlight's shining threads.

She watched as a procession of fireflies floated through the open windows. They flickered softly in the room's deep shadows, before venturing back out to join their brethren in the garden. It was really too early in the year for fireflies, but like the bees, they had been fooled into thinking it summer. She knew their twinkling lights could so easily be lost if another chill was to come. That worry sat heavily in her mind, and she said as much to the phooka.

"An understandable concern," he acknowledged, as he continued to weave a cat's cradle from the moonbeams in his hands. "Having seen what we've seen, and knowing what we know, the question now is, what is to be done? Or can we do anything at all?"

It was the same question she had been asking herself. "I don't have an answer," she admitted. "But I believe that only ill will come from doing nothing at all. There was truth in Thom's words when he said that our world no longer knows which way to turn, and that given time it will forget itself entirely, to our undoing."

"And what do you think of the boy's answer to that quandary?" he asked, lazily leaning forward as though he would slip the shining threads stretched between his fingers around her bare foot.

She pulled said foot out of his easy reach as a matter of course. In her mind's eye, she could clearly see Lorne and his bride dancing on the snow at Yule, and remembered how the world was made right around them. Absently she shifted her other foot away as the phooka continued to amuse himself with his game.

The Goblin King's lands were not dull as were those beholden to the exiled queen. And why should they be? Their king's heart was whole, made so by his love of Lumina. And of course, she had seen for herself that his lady's glade did not suffer under the same fate as the rest of the fairies' wood. Could the answer really be as simple as replacing one queen with another? She felt a tug at her hand and looked down to find it caught in the web of Hoax's weaving.

"You and your foolishness!" she said, shaking her hand to rid herself of the strands. They held tight, and she realized there was more to that weaving than just moonlight and empty promises. Her heart side-stepped from what that something more might be. "Don't you want an answer to your question?"

"I do." The layered meaning behind his words piled up like fallen leaves as he spoke them. "But I already know my answer, I am just waiting for you to find yours."

"Then I think we should ask your King's lady what her thoughts are before we have too many more of our own," she replied, choosing to answer the question at hand, ignoring any others the tricky rogue in front of her might be alluding to.

His thumb brushed over the back of her hand, sweeping away the strands of glittering moonlight. "Well, if that is the only answer you have to give, then I am off to do as you command." And with that, he donned his feathers.

She watched him wing his way out through the window. Her feelings twisted around inside her, as elusive as a cat's tail to the cat who was trying to catch it.

Her concerns from the night before were realized when the morning came. A cold wind had blown in from the far-off sea, and the trees bent their heads before it. Their tender young leaves, having just begun to grow again after the frost, shivered beneath the onslaught and tore loose from their moorings. Delicate petals were snatched from their new blossoms to be carried away by the marauding gale. On the heels of the wind came the White Stag with his tiny queen sitting amongst his silver antlers.

The eld woman opened the gate, greeting them as they passed through. The raven who had brought them glided past her, brushing his wingtips lightly over her hair as he did so. She scowled at his retreating tail feathers, more out of habit than true displeasure. Closing the gate, she headed back towards the cottage where her friends waited.

The raging wind had gentled some at their coming, so she set about opening the cottage's windows. This allowed the rose petals which had gathered outside on the sills to flutter in, much to her consternation and young Thom's delight.

A kettle was already on her new stove heating up for tea, and it was not long before she was seated at the table with everyone else, cup in hand.

"The wind feels strange today," Lorne observed, plucking a rose petal from the air before it could land in his tea.

"Much has been strange these past months," Lumina commented from where she sat in her customary seat atop the table. The tiny sprite smiled up at the eld woman as she accepted her unspoken offer of tea. "But, Hoax tells us that you may have some idea as to why that may be."

The eld woman nodded her head as she carefully poured more tea into the blue thimble in front of Lumina. "I do, though it would be better to say that Thom showed us a reason why things may be as they are."

"Thom showed you?" Lumina's tone was more surprised than disbelieving.

It was the phooka sitting at the table's head that answered. "He did. And led us a merry chase in the process. Down one of the old ways he took us, to a door that we once knew well, but had long since forgotten."

"If it is the doorway I think it to be, then the forgetfulness was by design." Lorne said, taking a slow sip of his tea.

"So it is, and so it was," The phooka quipped, but there was no humor in it. "The land on the other side, however, is not as it was. The court Underhill is a broken place now, filled with tarnished leaves and empty shadows."

"And you believe the reason for that is because it has lost its queen?" Lorne said in a tone that made it clear that he still had not forgiven the once Fairy Queen for past wrongs.

Lost, the word niggled at her brain. It called to mind an admission whispered to her in the dark. A memory of coolness washing over her fevered skin as quiet words, heavy with truth, were dressed in teasing tones and delivered lightly to her ears.

"Perhaps it is not that the land has lost its queen, but that the queen, herself, is lost." She felt the truth in her own words even as she spoke them, and could see understanding dawn in the eyes around her.

"And you believe this is why things are as they are?" Lumina asked.

"Yes," she confessed. "Thom said as much when we were standing amongst the shards of her throne. 'No dancers dance in the round, so the world no longer knows which way to turn'. The Fairy Queen's rounds no longer turn, so the seasons have lost their step and the world is showing us its displeasure. But what to do about it, that is a question I am not sure I have an answer for."

"Blue-Rose Woman loves to dance," said Thom from where he sat with the silver cat, catching rose petals as they drifted in on the wind.

"So I do," Lumina agreed, looking over and smiling at Thom. "Perhaps if we go to see this broken court, we may better be able to figure out what can be done to mend it."

They left shortly thereafter. The eld woman and Thom upon Hoax's back and Lumina on the White Stag's. The silver cat chose to take his own path, as was his habit.

They traveled down the old road just as they had the day before, passing by the ancient bridge and through the crossroads with its pillar of moonstone. They continued on until they were standing at the foot of the same bare green hill Thom had led Hoax and herself to the previous morning. The fairy mound looked just as it had then with its grassy head covered in little flowers that waved eagerly at them in the ceaseless wind. Except now there was no door to be seen in its verdant banks, wooden or otherwise.

She felt Thom slide down from where he rode behind her and watched him walk over to the unblemished hillside with steady purpose. Reaching out, he pushed at the place in front of him where the door should have been. The spot beneath the boy's hand remained stubbornly empty.

"The way won't open." The boy's words carried such a sadness in them that she was surprised that the whole world did not weep from it. Her own heart certainly ached hearing them.

Lumina slid from the White Stag's back and went over to stand next to the boy, reaching out to rest her own hand next to his. "It does seem well and truly shut," she agreed as the wind gave a hard tug at her moth-wing coat.

"Perhaps that is because the one to whom it still belongs does not want it opened," Hoax suggested. "One wonders if she knows that faerie is sinking softly into madness and taking the mortal world along with it, or whether she would care if she did."

The eld woman thought the phooka might have the right of it, at least in part. It was clear that Underhill still belonged to the exiled queen, and if it was her will that it remained closed then closed it would remain. Of his other speculations, she was not so sure.

"You think this is willful maliciousness on Maeve's part?" the White Stag asked his errant knight who shook his mane in response.

"How am I to know? The hearts of all queens are a mystery to me." Hoax danced in little springy steps beneath her. She smacked his brawny neck lightly without thinking, realizing her mistake immediately as she felt the rumble of laughter through her legs. "See! How is one to know when they hold you tightly and chastise you all in the same motion?"

"I think all of us here can admit to a certain confusion when it comes to matters of the heart," Lumina gently teased, all the while looking fondly over at the White Stag. "And though I know you will think me foolish; I do not believe that the Fairy Queen does this on purpose. In fact, I believe she does not even realize what is happening, and perhaps things could be made right if one of us were only to speak to her."

The White Stag brushed his muzzle gently against his bride's cheek. "You are kinder than I, my love. I would be willing to speak to her if you wished it, though I doubt she would be inclined to listen. In fact of all of us, I would be the one she was least likely to listen to. But whether she would or wouldn't is of no consequence, as I have not seen even a flash of her white flank since her doom was laid upon her."

"I could chase her down," Hoax suggested eagerly and the eld woman felt his muscles bunch and twitch in anticipation of the hunt.

"No," the White Stag was adamant. "I promised I would not send my hunt to haunt her heels, even though she had once sent hers to hound mine, and I will not go back on that."

"I made no such promise," she felt the need to point out. "And though Maeve is no more likely to listen to me than she is to you, I have one thing on my side that may prove useful. Of all of us, I can best understand the human heart."

"If you remember, Arianna, I too had a mortal heart once," the White Stag reminded her unnecessarily. "But I suppose that was a long time ago, if the phooka's wildly rolling eyes are any indication. Careful Hoax, you'll do yourself a mischief."

She laughed at their banter, though her skin prickled at the sound of her name spoken aloud. Names had power, and she had been called by so many others for so long that it felt as though her own name was a stranger to her.

That evening she sat in her garden with only herself for company, something that had not happened in a while. The wind had retreated, leaving little breezes behind to cavort through the gorse hedge in fits and spurts. Their antics caused the bells that hung there to chime in a most querulous manner.

Only a few fireflies ventured out into the cool twilight, but their numbers were made up for by the will-o-wisps that bobbed along beside them. The wards made by the hedge bells kept the other fair folk away but did little to keep those dancing lights out. They were mostly elementals after all, made up of salamander sparks traveling through the night air.

Her eyes followed them as they passed from her garden to the dark wood beyond, her mind mulling over all that had happened earlier that day; the assurances she had made to the Goblin King and the promises that had been given in return. Should the way open, Lorne and his lady would go under-the-hill and try to make right the damage that had been wrought. But it was on her to open the way, and that meant finding the white hind and making her see reason, two seemingly impossible tasks.

Actually, the first task did not worry her overly much. Unlike the Goblin King, she had at least seen the white hind, perhaps even more than once in retrospect. It was very possible the flash she had thought was the White Stag that day in the fairy wood, when they had gone a-milking, had actually been the white hind. And she was sure that the shadow she had seen on the door of the fairy mound had been hers as well. So, it stood to reason that she would see her again. No, it was certainly the second task that was the more daunting of the two.

Despite her earlier claims, she wondered if she truly could understand an immortal creature doomed with a mortal heart and all the desires and fears that came with it. For the fae, emotions were often fleeting, like waves moving across the water rather than the currents flowing within it. Those of mortals were deeper, richer and so much fuller, perhaps because their lives were measured in years rather than eons. She was sure that it was that feeling of life, with all its intoxicating emotion, that first drew the Fairy Queen to spirit away Tamlin and Lorne. She suspected that it was most likely the loss of that feeling that drove her to deceive Lumina in her efforts to draw Lorne back. And it was the desire for that feeling that had become the anchor for the curse that bound her now.

It was also that feeling, and all the confusion that came with it, that she hoped to use to convince the fallen queen to let go of her hold on faerie. Of course, she still had to accomplish the first task, before she could move on to the second.

She stayed where she was for a long while, watching as the moon rose and washed her garden in silver. Hoax was with Thom, and when last she checked they were playing a game whose rules she did not understand, if it had any rules at all.

Something brushed against her skirts. She looked down to find the silver cat watching her with big shining eyes. He had been about his own business for most of the day, as cats were wont to do, meeting them at the gate when they had returned home, only to leave again with his mistress when she had departed.

"I see you're back. Does your mistress no longer need you?" She asked, making room so that he could jump into her lap, which he did.

He kneaded her skirt with first one paw then the other. "Of course she still needs me, but she is dancing with the master in her garden. So, I decided to come back here. You still have that fish in the spring cellar."

She snorted softly, stroking the cat's moon-silvered fur. "So I do," she said, smoothing his whiskers with the backs of her fingers, first one side then the other. "Tell me, do you know where the white hind is?"

"No, but I know where she will be. Sleep in tomorrow morning and you will too."

The next morning, she did as the silver cat suggested, quietly lingering in the bed that had been gifted to her. She had taken to sleeping in it after her illness, seeing no reason not to at that point.

As the room brightened in the early morning light, she saw Thom rise from his bed and make his way over to the window she so often found him looking out of. She shifted slowly in her bed so that she might catch a glimpse of what it was that held him in such thrall.

This time she could clearly see the hind, its coat white

as thorn, staring back at Thom from the deep shadows of the woods. Its lovely head was held up high on its graceful neck; large ears, delicate as porcelain, were turned in their direction with unwavering attention. It stood that way for a long while, then it was gone, vanished as though it had never been.

At that moment many things fell into place, including how she could trap the fallen queen.

CHAPTER 6

Crowning of the May Queen

She walked through her garden in the morning's dazzling light. Flowers bloomed all around her, determined to grow despite the late frosts and punishing winds they had endured. Much like love, came a sudden thought, unbidden.

The first day of May was nearly upon them and for some unfathomable reason that knowledge brought with it a sense of urgency to complete the tasks set for her. She had been careful to watch Thom after having seen the white hind in the woods beyond her window, and had been rewarded with the knowledge that the white hind did indeed visit nearly every morning. It made her wonder if the exiled queen had a choice or if it was something that she was compelled to do, like a moth drawn to a flame.

Whatever the truth may be, she now knew where to find the white hind. But what to do with that knowledge?

She continued about the business of filling her gathering basket with nettles and yarrow. Her garden was not one of order, but rather contained wildness, filled with twisting paths that grew of their own accord. It drew you in deeper towards its center, to where Old Man Apple stood surrounded by his progeny, a small orchard of apple trees that were ancient, yet still saplings when compared with their parent. But this morning those paths had led her to the edge of a large bed of clover. It was a favorite place of Thom's, who was laying there even now, watching the clouds as he often did.

Looking at him lying there, a whisper of an idea ghosted through her thoughts. She now felt she knew how to draw the white hind to a place where she could reason with her, and where that place might be, but the how of keeping her there still eluded her.

She continued on to where Hoax sat not far away, beneath the linden tree. Setting her basket down, she sat on the stone seat beside him. He was amusing himself by playing with shadows, fashioning them into little mazes. She watched him spin them into webs and spirals, trapping little bits of light in their hearts. His fingers were as deft at weaving shadows into patterns as they had been at making moonlight into cat's cradles. She could still remember the tug of the threads as they gently held her hand fast.

It would take something very special to capture a creature such as the white hind. Something that would hold, but not harm; something that could hold that which was not meant to be held.

"Tell me Hoax, how do you weave a net to catch the wind?"

"With love, of course."

There was something in his answer, something profound that stared back at her with patient eyes.

It set her heart pounding and her mind awhirl. As she struggled to comprehend a truth that her heart already understood, another thought pushed its way to the fore. In that flash of clarity, she knew exactly how they would go about snaring the white hind.

It would have to be Thom's hand that set the trap. Guilt pricked at her with that thought. She knew that using him in such a way would be a betrayal of his trust in her, and the white hind's trust in him. That understanding did not make her happy, and she said as much to the phooka beside her.

She noticed the sardonic smile that played softly along the goblin's lips and wondered at it. "Ask him," he said. "Thom sees things clearly, sometimes clearer than you do."

The whole day passed by and still she could not find the words she needed. It was no small thing to ask a person to betray someone they loved. And she had no doubt that Thom loved the Fairy Queen. Whether it was of his own volition or not though, that she could not say.

A storm blew in that night, unlooked for, which suited her needs perfectly. She went out into the pelting rain in only her shift, for practicality reasons more than any other, since the thin fabric would dry the quickest by the fire. The wind sang loudly around her as she endeavored to capture the wild rain in the silver bowl she was holding just for that purpose. It would have taken longer if some playful sylphs had not made a game of catching raindrops for her. They swirled past on the back of the eddying winds, laughing as they tossed their offerings into the waiting bowl.

She did not return to the house until it was over half full. Hoax knew what she was about and met her at the door, a cloth for her to dry off with in hand. He wrapped it around her as best he could before taking the bowl from her so that she might go change into her other shift.

When she came out, she found the silver bowl waiting for her on the table. Next to it was the skein of spider's thread which had been among the many purchases that Hoax and the silver cat had made during her illness. The phooka had not lit the oil lamps, instead leaving the candles to stand sentry in each window. Their steadfast flames filled the house with light and the smell of beeswax as the rain drummed heartily against the glass.

Hoax had already pulled her wing chair closer to the stove. He and the boy were sitting as they often did now before bed, Hoax stretched out on the rug in front of her chair with the boy sitting close by. Tonight, Thom was playing with a long piece of string, which the silver cat would occasionally catch with his paw, when the temptation became too much for him. Usually, she would be sitting with them, her hair undone as she combed it dry. It had become something of a habit for them to sit like that of an evening, and she found that she had come to look forward to it. Her heart would be perfectly content to have such quiet moments continue on far into the future. Unfortunately, this night there was other business which had to be attended to.

"Thom," she called his name and waited for him to look at her. When he did, she gestured for him to join her near the table. He came over readily enough to see what it was that she had laid out there. "I need to speak with the white hind and she must stay to listen. Will you help me make a place that she will not be able to leave until I have spoken to her? I promise I will do her no harm, nor will I hold her longer than needed."

He looked at the bowl and thread on the table for a long while and she waited patiently for his answer. Finally, he turned his bright gaze on her. His blue-green eyes looked straight into hers, something he almost never did. She wondered what it was that he looked for, or if he even understood what it was that she was asking.

Eventually, he slowly nodded his head once. "I will," he said.

She gently brushed her hand over his golden head. "Thank you."

She went to reach for the skein of spider's thread only to find it gone. Thom held out his hands so that she could see the shimmering web woven between his fingers. She held out the bowl and he slid the weaving into the waiting water. She then placed it in a spot that she knew saw the sky so that she might catch the moon in her silver bowl once the storm had passed.

They returned to the warmth of the stove. She sank into the waiting wing chair while Thom settled on the cushion next to her, his head on her knee. The tiredness that had become more absent of late fell heavily on her, and she greeted it with open arms, sliding down into sleep amongst the unbound tangle of her rain-soaked hair.

It was full dark when she woke, her cheek comfortably resting on sheets warmed from her own body heat and that of the creature draped across her feet. It was no mystery as to how she had gotten there, but she was slightly perplexed to find her hair brushed smooth and neatly braided. Grateful for the kindness, she reached down and gently stroked the hound's ears, smiling as she did so. Perhaps she should be more appreciative of goblins and their goblin ways.

Time enough to think of that later. The coming day would not be an easy one and there was still much to do. She slipped quietly out of bed and went about preparing for what needed to be done.

She and Thom were out in the garden long before the sun had shown itself. A shimmering mist filled the silver bowl she carried; the result of the spider's thread and the storm waters' contrivances in the moonlight. She instructed Thom to wash in the swirling opalescence, watching as it settled like diamond dust on the boy's hands.

That done, they began to move through the garden, starting at the gate and walking slowly alongside the gorse hedge that served as the garden's boundary. Thom followed her example, touching everywhere she would touch. The bells in the hedge quietened in their wake as they made their full way around.

It took them quite a while, the whole of the garden being nearly half the size of the village where she had once been called a wise woman, so very long ago. They followed the same path she had walked just the day before until they reached the patch of clover that Thom enjoyed so much.

The sun had only just lifted its head over the horizon when she left him there, stretched out in the dew. She headed back to the house, and a short while later she and Hoax left, heading out across the moors.

The day grew brighter. The rising sun smiled brightly down on the heavily dewed plants. Its light shone through every water droplet, fragmenting into impossibly brilliant colors so that each stem, branch and leaf was encrusted with rainbows.

The white hind leapt boldly over the now silent hedge. Her lithe form ghosted over the ground, treading so lightly that the dewdrops did not even shiver at her passing. When she reached the place where Thom lay, she lowered her muzzle, touching him gently over his heart.

In that instant, every drop of dew fell with a clamor of bells, and the boy vanished. The colors of before disappeared along with the seeming of Thom. The white hind's muscles bunched as she made to flee, but despite her obvious attempt, she did not move from the spot where she stood.

The eld woman stepped from the cottage and looked with dispassionate eyes at the beautiful creature stuck fast in the web of invisible thread. She walked along the familiar paths to the spot where the white hind stood unmoving, her regal head held high.

The eld woman made herself comfortable on the stone seat beneath the linden tree. "There is much that I need to discuss with you," she said, meeting the exiled queen's wary gaze. "Mostly to do with the disruption in the world around us of late, which even you could not have failed to notice."

The doe lowered her head to the spot where the illusion of the boy had lain. A mournful sound filled the air between them. It was the same heart-wrenching sound the white hind had made when her doom had first fallen full upon her, the same one the eld woman had heard again later that night when Thom had come to stay in her house at the wood's edge.

"It was his *fetch* that lay there, not him. An illusion, meant to draw you here. Did it never occur to you that this may have been a trap? Of course not, what would you know of such things save the ones that you, yourself, have laid?"

The white hind still said nothing, only looked at her with confusion and hopelessness in her eyes. Something occurred to the eld woman then.

"Have you lost your voice, Maeve? Has your mortal heart thrown you into such a state that you no longer have the power of speech?"

The doe lowered her head once in acknowledgment.

The eld woman's own heart softened a little. "It is true that there is no love lost between us. But of all those we know, at this moment I am the one who can understand you best. So I will share with you a secret. If you had no love for the boy then the net we wove would not have held you.

"It is most likely that feeling which has plagued you and robbed you of your speech. A longing that preys on your mind, turning the heart in your chest into a lode-stone that pulls at you constantly. But I can tell you that it does not always feel so. That feeling which you have can bring light to your world, transform it into so much more than it was. Lorne knows this, perhaps more than anyone. It was not a curse that he placed on you, but rather your heart's wish that he granted. Whether you realize it or not, it was what you were seeking all along but did not understand."

The white hind's head came up and the eld woman stopped, turning to look in the same direction. She saw a streak of gold, followed by one of black, racing down the garden paths towards them. The gold was Thom, who stopped his headlong dash abruptly as soon as he came up alongside her. The black was Hoax, of course, who came panting up next to her.

"He would not be stopped," he explained to her as he flopped down on his hound's haunches. "It was like he was driven by a demon."

"Fairy-driven more like," the eld woman said. Now that she knew to look for it, she could see a web of diamond-bright threads stretching out between the fallen queen and the boy. They glittered in her sight, hard and unyielding amongst the deep red threads that tied Thom to the phooka and herself. They explained much of what had driven the boy to do as he had done this past half-year.

Hoax growled, quieting only when Thom reached over to place his hand on the phooka's ruff. He turned his snarling visage on the trapped queen.

"I would run you to ground, save this boy's wishes and my king's command," vowed the phooka. "There would be no rest for you, just as there was none for my liege. He gave you his heart and you blinded him for it and sent your hunt to hound his every step. This boy has done the same and you tie him to you, so that he will search you out barefooted in the snow or through rivers swollen with rains.

"Do you care what things might happen to his mortal shell? That he is trapped just as you are now?" Hoax's words did not twist or turn as they were want to do, instead they cut sharply at the white hind. "To love someone is to put their needs above your own. To be their eyes when they need to see, their hands when they cannot care for themselves. To do this freely because your own heart demands that you do, not because a geas compels you to."

The white hind shivered, finally finding the voice she had lost. "What has your king done to me?" she moaned, the anguish of a hundred dying angels ringing out in her plea.

"He has given you what it was that you sought. If you would truly know love, free the boy, Maeve. Free Underhill so that the world might be set to rights," the eld woman implored the fallen queen gently. "Accept your curse and understand it to be the gift that it is."

"I have no wish to understand it!" the hind cried out and this time when she went to leap away, she could. The glittering strands of the geas fell away between her and the boy, freeing him. Only a single golden thread stretched, shining between them. That one the fallen queen could not break, and the eld woman knew *she* certainly would not break it. It was not her place to deny fate.

On the very last evening of April, a laughing Lady of the Glade came to the eld woman's door with flowers in her hair. She came hand in hand with the Goblin King, to chivvy all in the house into coming with her, and she would not be denied. So up onto Hoax's pony back the eld woman went with Thom, to follow where the golden-eyed lady led.

All through the goblin wood they danced, the Goblin King and his merry lady. The wood resounded in their wake with the clopping of hooves and the clatter of shells and sound of bells cheerfully ringing. It was the sound of the Goblin Host heeding the call of their lord and lady.

Swaying lanterns twinkled in the evening shade, making double all those who sang and played, setting free their shadows to caper amongst the darkling trees. Beneath them, the phooka danced with a great flashing of hooves. But no matter how he dipped or sidled, his riders never had cause for fear.

Down the ancient road the fairy rade traveled, as it hadn't in many a long year. Through the crossroads with its pillar of moonstone and over the crumbling bridge they gamboled in their revelry. The eld woman, perched atop the phooka's back, recognized the dell of forget-me-nots when they came upon it. Thrice around the old stone well they ringed before making their winding way through the thick boles of wych-elm and oak.

Over hills and through shaded vales the merry-makers went until they came to the border stream. It rushed angrily through its still swollen banks, but that did not stop the golden-eyed lady with her silver-antlered king. A bridge of mist and moonlight came to be beneath their dancing feet. They crossed over the snapping water with nary a qualm, and their host came in close attendance after.

The drowned meadow greeted them on the far bank, its flowers waving joyfully above their watery feet. Here the nixy from the lake joined them as did many others of the fairy court. Their swirling laughter called even the Rowan Maiden to leave her young tree for a while and dance with them.

In the glade, they found tables laden with food. Great fires licked at the sky with tongues of violet and gold. The salamanders at their hearts, as tall as men, spun and leapt wildly through the pyre, sending their light out into the night.

The eld woman slid from the phooka's back, helping Thom down after her. No sooner had their feet touched the ground then she saw the familiar sight of Meg coming towards them. The gruagach's green hair was filled with flowers as though they had bloomed from her locks, and her eyes were alive with joy. She hugged them all then took Thom's hand, leading him over to where the young rowan tree stood, the silver cat already draped across its rooty foot. There she sat Thom down on velvet cushions beneath the sapling's thin branches. Her heart lightened at seeing him settled and safe in Meg's care.

The Goblin King had made himself a fiddle and was playing a wild tune. His lady put her feet to the rhythm, the new beginnings of Spring in her every step.

Hoax took her hand in his. "Come dance with me!" She opened her mouth to reply only to find his finger against her lips. "*Tch, tch,* I know what it is you are about to say. And I would say in return that there is no need to fear being led astray for it already happened so long ago that it's well past time to fret about it."

"And who is making assumptions now!" she said, brushing his finger away. "I was going to say yes, had you but given me the chance, you infuriating phooka."

"Well then, damn my foolish tongue!" he laughed and swept her up into the dance.

Hoax held her as they danced, from firelight to moonlight and back again. The world became a thing of color and music, a dizzying whirl whose only constant was a pair of green eyes that never stopped smiling at her. She danced as she had danced when she was still young and new.

But, she was not young or new. And she was mortal yet, so it did not take long before her feet began to flag. The phooka knew, of course, and without her having to say a word. He led them to a dry place where they could rest just beyond the fire's light. There they sat amongst the moon-silvered flowers, her head resting on his shoulder as they watched the others frolic.

It came that another fiddler took up the tune. The Goblin King joined his lady in the round and the world grew brighter for it. A great sigh gusted softly past her ear as those two dear figures moved through the flickering dark. It was filled with a longing that she had not expected.

"You have asked me more than once if I loved him," she said, unsure of what she was asking even as she asked it. "But I have never thought to ask you."

"It is true. I do love him," he admitted. "I love her as well, unashamedly. How could I not? The world itself loves them. But I feel as though you have once again misunderstood my meaning, and I am beginning to wonder if you do it willfully. Let me reassure you that I do not watch them with a lustful eye, or rather I do, for I lust after what they have found and that I still wish for."

Her heart thumped once, hard, and though she had no intention of asking the question, her lips asked it anyways. "What is it you wish for?"

"I have told you this before," he sighed, and she could not help but be amused as it seemed for once it was the phooka who was exasperated rather than herself.

"Have you?" she asked, enjoying herself despite the shiver that raced over her skin and made her belly tremble. His shoulder moved as he leaned over, resting his cheek against hers so that she could feel the wicked smile bloom across his face.

"Many, many times. But it seems that you have not been listening. So let me say it plainly, here beneath the sky for all the stars to witness. I love you."

Her world exploded and was born anew. He laughed gently at her as she drew back and stared at him.

"How can this be such a surprise? We have been friends for so long, how could you not have known? And you call me foolish! But I suppose I am, for my heart grows lighter with every scowl and admonishment you send my way. So, one could say that you only have yourself to blame for my foolishness. Oh, don't look at me with those daggers in your eyes. I might cut myself, for I cannot look away!"

She felt as though she were falling, as he leaned forward again. His warm breath on her cheek was as familiar as her own reflection.

"Give me your name, Arianna," he breathed. "Whisper it in my ear and I'll whisper mine in yours."

Terror and elation warred inside her as she breathed, "It is already there on your tongue."

"But you have never given it to me."

It sat there on her lips, trembling like a dewdrop just before the fall. And just as that dewdrop, there would be no recovering it once it did.

The great tolling of a bell sounded throughout the glade, and her name remained unspoken. A golden light spilled out from beyond the silvery beeches, washing over the bluebells like the morning sun over the sea. With a joyous shout, the revelers, one and all, made their way towards it.

Hoax fell back into the flowers as though he had been struck. "It seems that I am destined to be thwarted," he lamented, then hopped to his feet, his attention fixing on two figures who were making their way towards them. "But I am nothing if not persistent."

Meg arrived then, with Thom in tow. "The way is open," the boy said, a light shining in his eyes.

"So it seems, my boy," the phooka agreed, taking up one of Thom's hands while offering his other to her stunned self still sitting on the ground. "Shall we see what there is to see?"

The hazel grove was awash with golden light. It poured forth from the cleft boulder like a sunrise, evidence that when the fallen queen had set Thom free, she had also relinquished her hold on faerie and its doorway to Underhill. The eld woman felt a twinge of pity for Maeve, and for how they had played on her new emotions to bring about this end. However, her conscience could not plague her too much, given the results. She wondered if Maeve herself knew why she had done what she did, or if perhaps the once Fairy Queen believed that she was freeing herself from those things that set those emotions crashing around inside her. The eld woman doubted that she would ever know the answer.

The Goblin King and his Lady stepped into the beckoning light and a long string of merrymakers followed, a twisting turning line with them at the tail.

The eld woman was gladdened by the sight that greeted her. Tarnished leaves still covered the ground, but above them new ones grew, in shining copper and gold. The land they walked through was no longer the desolate place it had been. It sparked with new life, and with that new life came the return of all the reasons there were warnings about dealing with faerie that mortals should take heed of.

She could feel the music drawing her in as it had not before, promising her things that she did not even know to ask for. Figures of shadow and light danced amongst the crystal trees, and they called to her to join them.

A hand fell over her eyes, blocking the sight from her view.

"This land is too awake now to be safe for you," said the phooka. "More's the pity."

Sleep stole over her on swift feet and she felt herself falling, drifting as gently as a dandelion seed on the wind.

She woke the next morning to the sight of a smiling phooka sitting next to her, chin in hand. He was dressed all in green from head to toe with the new leaves of spring woven throughout the dark waves of his hair.

"The Queen of May has opened her eyes and the sun shines all the brighter for it," he said, bringing a strand of her silver banded hair up to his lips from where it lay unbound in the sweet-smelling grass. A crown of flowers had been placed on her head, and the petals hanging down from it conspired to frame all the world in springtime.

The Queen of May, indeed, she thought, but found that she could not even summon up a scowl to send his way. The confessions that he had made to her the night before still shone in his eyes as he looked down at her, and she could not deny that she had been foolish not to see it before.

"Thom is still with Meg, so there is no need to worry," he assured her. "What's more, his heart seems to be content in a way it has not been until now."

She closed her eyes as she felt the world around her settle. The loneliness and worry did not ride her as it had because she knew herself not to be alone. The lost ones were no longer lost, having found their home in each other.

"You know, you promised me a name," said the phooka, close to her ear.

"And when did I do that?" she asked, chuckling as she opened her eyes to look up into his.

"Why your heart promised it to me last night, but your lips were too shy to speak it," he said. "No matter, I will give you mine, since my heart has been yours all along."

There beneath the smiling sun, his name fell from his lips into her ear, and she breathed hers into his.

EPILOGUE

Midsummer's Eve

The night air was warm and soft, and the stars above had made themselves into a glittering blanket for the dusky sky.

Hoax and Thom stood next to her in the dark, watching as the fairy mound rose up on its golden pillars as it hadn't in many centuries. Music and light poured forth from under the hill, and if they were to look just right, they could see past the crystal trees to where the Goblin King and the Lady of the Glade danced. The rings of dancers, greater and lesser, spun around them, turning in their eternal wheels, setting the worlds to right once more.

As for the eld woman, she let the sight wash over her, through her, then let it go. Even for mortals like herself and Thom, it was best to think of what they saw as just a dream, lest it overshadow the beauty that could be had in the mortal world. Which was a truer beauty to her mind than that of the other.

When they turned towards home, they found the white hind in their path. She stood there, bright as a rising moon, shivering with some great emotion that it was clear she did not understand. The eld woman found that she no longer held any animosity in her heart for the poor lost queen. Queen no longer, really, for Maeve had given up her court and her realm so that the world could be made whole.

Thom stepped away from them, walking ahead to where the beautiful creature waited; his hand held out towards her. There was no longer a geas compelling him to do so, only sympathy and his own great heart. The white hind took a hesitant step towards him, looking as though she wanted something, but unsure of what that something was.

They stood there, frozen in that timeless moment, as the eld woman and Hoax watched on. Then the wind rustled through the trees, and the hind shied away from Thom's hand. Her eyes were wide as she looked at him, and the eld woman fancied that she could see a kaleidoscope of emotions reflected within them. The white hind turned and fled into the forest where the darkness swallowed her up.

The eld woman turned to look at Hoax beside her. His green eyes, luminous in the waxing moon, looked thoughtfully in the direction in which the white hind had disappeared.

"It may be that it'll take some time, but I believe that their story is not yet done," he mused, the expression on his face thoughtful, and a much kinder one than she would have expected him to have for the creature who had just left.

"I am sure you are right," she said, taking his hand in hers. "Perhaps neither is ours." Then she grinned because the wide eyes he turned towards her told her that for once her incorrigible phooka had been struck dumb.

It did not last long, of course. He laughed and spun her round and before she knew it, he had kissed her soundly.

"No, most assuredly my sweet Arianna, ours is just beginning," he promised as he kissed her again.

A soft warmth filled her other hand, and she looked down to find Thom smiling up at her.

"Time to go home," he said to her.

"Yes, love, it is time for all of us to go home."

The End

Endnotes

1. Francis James Child, "Tam Lin 39A," *The English and Scottish Popular Ballads* (1882-1898)

AUTHOR'S NOTE

Stories often have a mind of their own, don't they? Take *Lumina and the Goblin King*; I had really only ever planned on it being a stand-alone book. Then, as I was writing the epilogue it came to me that there were more stories to be told. That even happy endings aren't really endings at all, just the beginnings of new stories. The banter between Hoax and the eld woman grew of its own accord with very little help from me, and I realized as I was writing it that their interaction was more than just verisimilitude for Lumina's story.

Also, I will admit that, being of a certain age and somewhat prickly nature, I have a feeling of kinship with the eld woman. I too understand the trials and maelstrom of emotions that come with taking care of a child that doesn't fit with the norm. Although Thom was not modeled off of my daughter, she certainly provided a great deal of inspiration for my writing of the little fairy-lost boy whose story is also not yet finished.

And as always, to the two loves of my life, my husband and our daughter, thank you for all that you are and all that you do. I also want to thank my steadfast friend Jenni. Your unwavering support means more than you can know. And a huge thank you to my mother as well who helps in myriad ways both big and small and never once told me not to make up stories.